"Who are yo[...]

"My name is Gra[...]

"You've explained [...] with exaggerated patience. "What are you doing here?"

He slid one hand into his pocket, further stretching the fabric of his slacks over his muscular thighs. Merry kept her eyes trained fiercely on Grant's face. "I came to talk to you about the party you're arranging for my sister."

"Oh, I'm so sorry." Merry felt her cheeks going deep red. "Why didn't you tell me?"

"Hey, don't apologize." Grant chuckled. "I could have explained, but then I realized I was having fun."

"You were having fun taking dictation and typing letters?"

"You bet." The deep creases at the corners of his mouth deepened with his grin. "And tomorrow I'll be back for more…"

Special thanks to Sheila Glasscock of *Celebration!*, a division
of Glasscock Convention Services, Little Rock, Arkansas;
and to Dorothy Sweaney, Heritage Book Store, Springfield,
Missouri.

❦

GINA WILKINS
is also the author of these novels in *Temptation*:

HERO IN DISGUISE
HERO FOR THE ASKING
HERO BY NATURE
A BRIGHT IDEA
A STROKE OF GENIUS
COULD IT BE MAGIC
CHANGING THE RULES
AFTER HOURS
A REBEL AT HEART
A PERFECT STRANGER
HOTLINE
*TAKING A CHANCE ON LOVE
*DESIGNS ON LOVE
*AT LONG LAST LOVE
WHEN IT'S RIGHT
RAFE'S ISLAND
AS LUCK WOULD HAVE IT
JUST HER LUCK
GOLD AND GLITTER
UNDERCOVER BABY
I WON'T!

*Veils & Vows trilogy

CAUSE FOR CELEBRATION

BY

GINA WILKINS

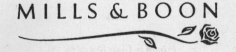

MILLS & BOON

*MILLS & BOON and the Rose Device are trademarks of the publisher.
TEMPTATION is a trademark of Harlequin Enterprises II B.V., used
under licence.
First published in Great Britain 1996
by Harlequin Mills & Boon Limited, Eton House, 18-24 Paradise Road,
Richmond, Surrey TW9 1SR*

© Gina Wilkins 1988

ISBN 0 263 79947 6

21 - 9608

*Printed in Great Britain by
BPC Paperbacks Ltd*

Prologue

"To Futron Inc. May it rest in peace."

"Futron's not dead, Tim. It's now a part of CMA Enterprises."

"Then here's to us. Two guys who started a little computer company in a closet-size office just when the computer revolution was getting into full swing. We worked our butts off, made a success of it, and now we've sold out for an obscene amount of money. We're free men, Grant, old boy. Retired at the young age of thirty-four."

"Speak for yourself. I'm not retiring. Unlike you, I'd go nuts lying on beaches all day with empty-headed bikini bunnies. I don't ever want to fall back into that trap of being so wrapped up in a job that there's no time for anything else in my life, but I've been giving some thought to what I want to do, businesswise. Thanks to CMA, I've got enough money to take my time and enjoy myself while I'm making my choice."

Though he looked surprised and a bit intrigued that Grant was already planning new businesses when his first "vacation" in years had barely begun, Grant's ex-partner sighed and made a quick motion with the crystal wineglass he'd been holding in the air. "Well, dammit, we're supposed to be celebrating. Let's make a toast to *something*.

Grant Bryant lifted his own glass and touched it to his friend's. "To wealthy freedom."

"Amen." Tim grinned, his dark blue eyes sparkling beneath the boyish lock of auburn hair that had fallen over his forehead.

Grant returned the grin and reached for a third slice of the enormous pizza with everything that rested on the table between them. The former owners of Futron Inc. were indulging in a private celebration of their success. Seated at the dining table in Tim's small but luxurious apartment, they reflected complacently on their good fortune.

After thirteen years of total absorption in Futron, sixteen hours a day, six or seven days a week, the two men had chosen to sell out to a megacorporation, giving them the financial means to pursue some of the pleasures they'd had no time for in the past years. Now there was time. Time to play, time to meet new challenges, time to fall in love and start families. Though neither of them would have spoken those thoughts, each knew the other shared similar hopes for the future, despite their teasing to the contrary. They were young, they were intelligent, they were free and they were ready for changes.

"So you still going to spend a couple of weeks with Leida in Missouri?" Tim asked. Leida was Grant's older sister. Divorced for several years, she adored her much younger brother and had asked both Grant and Tim to visit her when they were free.

Grant nodded, savoring the flavors of pizza and wine. "Yeah. I told her it would be at least three weeks before I could get there, but it looks like we're going to wrap up here quicker than we'd expected, so I may surprise her by showing up a week early."

"You're just trying to get there in time to stop her from throwing a party in your honor. You've hated that idea ever since she mentioned it."

Grant grimaced. "You're right. The woman will throw a party at the slightest provocation. I have no desire to be her next guest of honor."

"Good luck. Leida can be one determined woman when she sets her mind on something."

"You're telling me? Her poor, oft-victimized little brother?" Ignoring Tim's snort of disbelief at Grant's description of his solid, five-foot-ten frame as "little," Grant took another sip of wine and lowered his glass with a smug smile. "This time I've made up my mind. There will be no party."

"Sounds like famous last words to me," Tim muttered around a mouthful of food. Then he swallowed and grinned. "Be sure and have Leida send me an invitation, will you, old boy?"

He only laughed when Grant threw a napkin at him and reached for yet another slice of pizza.

THE CREATIVELY LETTERED sign over the door said MerryMakers. In smaller letters beneath, it informed anyone who was interested that the company specialized in planning, decorating and fully servicing theme parties. Grant scowled at the sign, then pushed open the door with a look of sheer determination on his strongly carved face.

Earlier that morning, during breakfast with his sister and her son, Grant had discovered that, sure enough, Leida planned to make him guest of honor at a party she had arranged through MerryMakers, just as Grant and Tim had suspected. She'd managed to keep it a secret for the week he'd been visiting her, but Chip, Grant's nephew, had let something slip that had led to Grant's finding out about MerryMakers.

Damned if he was going to let Leida put him on display like a prize pig, Grant fumed, stepping into the office reception area. Leida would probably throw a tantrum when she found out, but Grant had every intention of canceling that party right now. He'd always been a man to make snap decisions and then act on them. That trait had stood him well in the business world, putting him a step ahead of those who had to stop and consider all the ramifications. He intended it to help him now, by getting him out of this ridiculous party before it was too late to stop it. All he had to do was to convince these people that he was acting on Leida's authority. If it took a bribe, fine. He'd gladly pay it. He'd confront his sister with his fait accompli when she returned home from work that evening, when it would be too late for her to do anything about it.

Inside the brightly colored reception area of MerryMakers he found pandemonium. Telephones buzzed, a slender, dark-haired man argued heatedly with a pretty teenager and a coffee-skinned young man wearing a Drury College sweatshirt carried a stack of piñatas across the small reception area. Grant blinked. Yes, they were piñatas, at least half a dozen of assorted shapes and colors. And over the shoulder of his sweatshirt the fellow wore a gaily striped serape.

"Uh, excuse me," Grant began, hoping to attract someone's attention.

Pausing at the door, the serape-clad youth looked Grant over with inquisitive brown eyes. "Help you?" he asked, mumbling around a paper-shrouded donkey.

"My name is Grant Bryant," Grant said, not quite sure how to explain his purpose at this company. "Leida Carmichael—"

"Oh, Leida sent you," the young man interrupted. He grinned. "You're not exactly what we expected, but I'm glad you're here, anyway. This place is going to pieces without Marsha. Just go in that open office behind the reception desk. Merry's expecting you."

"But—"

"Get the door, will you, mister? This stuff's heavy, and I'm kinda in a hurry."

Resignedly Grant opened the door and the youth hurried out. What kind of place is this, anyway? Grant asked himself as he approached the desk where the dark-haired man still argued with the strawberry-blond teenager. Both were standing, facing each other angrily, both ignoring the approaching man as well as the buzzing telephone.

"Excuse me," Grant began.

"I mean it, Melinda. I don't want you going out with that delinquent again. You've just turned fourteen and he's nearly eighteen, and I won't have it." His attractive face flushed, the young man, who looked to be in his mid-twenties, glared down at the girl.

Melinda tossed her thick fall of curls out of her equally flushed and very pretty face to return the glare unblinkingly. "I will go out with anyone I want to, Matthew James, and I won't let you tell me I can't even if you are my older brother! Merry said I could date Savage, and *she's* my legal guardian, not you!"

Grant tried speaking a little louder. "Excuse me."

"Savage! What kind of a name is that, anyway? If you honestly think you can—"

"Would the two of you please shut up?" another voice yelled from behind them. "Melinda, Merry said you'd better answer the phone or you're fired."

Grant looked hopefully toward the door, then blinked—a gesture that was rapidly becoming a habit in this Twilight Zone of a business. The girl who'd come from the open office behind the desk was an exact duplicate of the strawberry blond, down to the identical black bows they wore in their fashionably shaggy hair. Same big green eyes, same pouty red mouth, same strong chin. Grant had no idea how anyone would possibly be able to tell them apart. In their matching black-and-hot-pink tunics over hot-pink tights, the girls were enough to make a sober man question his vision. "Excuse me," he almost shouted into the sudden silence.

Three pairs of startled green eyes turned in his direction, for all the world as if Grant were the one acting oddly. He felt an unaccustomed tinge of color stain his lean cheeks.

"May I help you, sir?" the newly arrived twin asked politely as the first—Melinda—finally answered the telephone, ignoring the fact that her brother still scowled at her.

"My name is Grant Bryant," he said again. "Leida Carmichael—"

"Oh, she sent a man!" the girl broke in with a dazzling smile. "What a nice change. Merry will love it. Just go on in."

Grant took a deep breath and tried to hang on to his waning patience. He had no idea who Merry was, but she couldn't be any less help than the four people he'd encountered so far in this nuthouse, he figured. Warily circling the desk, he approached the open office.

A woman with dark hair sat behind a desk, almost hidden behind stacks of paper, brochures, brightly colored posters and banners and—Grant had to look twice to make sure—a saddle, half covered by papers, one stirrup dangling down the side of the desk. And then the woman looked up at him with a smile and Grant wouldn't have noticed if a horse had suddenly appeared from beneath the desk.

He guessed her age to be mid-to-late twenties. Straight, dark brown hair—the rich, true brown of semisweet chocolate—swept over from a low part on the right side of her head and fell sleekly to turn under at her shoulders, with wispy bangs across her forehead. Her small face was slightly on the square side, softened by an absurdly pointed little chin and a short, elfin nose. Her smile tilted just a little, so that the dimple on the left side of her mouth dipped deeper than the one on the right. Her teeth were very even and very white, and her full

lower lip glistened moistly. Kissable. And her eyes...
Lord, what eyes! Almond shaped, fringed in black,
bright and lively and a deep, enticing green. The color
of fresh mint leaves, he decided, immediately developing a craving for chocolate mint.

The faintest of flushes tinted the woman's smooth
cheeks as Grant continued to stare at her, stunned by the
entrancing sight before him. "Hello," she greeted him, her
voice musical in the noticeable silence. "May I help you?"

Grant swallowed painfully, his Adam's apple bobbing in his strong, tanned neck. *I certainly hope so.* He
cleared his throat to keep himself from blurting out that
thought, then tried one more time to explain his mis-
sion. "My name is Grant Bryant. Leida Carmichael—"

"Oh, Leida sent you!" the woman interrupted in pleasure. "She told me she had a couple of men on staff now.
You don't know how glad I am to see you. You're late, but
that's okay. I just hope you're prepared to work fast."

Trying to ignore that innocently provocative phrase,
Grant reflected in exasperation that he'd completed exactly one sentence since he'd entered this place. He'd said
"My name is Grant Bryant" three times now. He was beginning to feel like one of those talking dolls with a stuck
string. "Actually, I—"

"Oh, good." The woman sighed in relief, brushing a
strand of hair away from her face and smiling at him in
a way that had his Adam's apple bobbing again. "This
place is just hopeless without Marsha." She located a
steno pad and pencil in the disaster of her desk and stood
to extend them to him. "There are three letters that must
go out this afternoon, and I have at least a dozen calls to
make in the next hour. Have these letters in the mail by
five and I'll love you forever," she breathed fervently.

That should just about do it, Grant thought dazedly, taking the pad and pencil without even noticing his actions. He thought he'd do just about anything to have this woman love him forever. He hoped his grin wasn't completely idiotic as he looked down at the top of her head, noting that she stood above five feet nothing in her neat little gray pumps. Just right for his own five feet ten inches. He also couldn't help noticing that she had a dynamite figure beneath her gray-and-pink plaid dress, despite her lack of inches. His fingers curled around the pencil to prevent them from reaching out to touch her.

She dropped back into her chair and waved toward a second chair beside the desk. "Make yourself comfortable," she told him. "Sorry I don't have a larger chair to offer you. By the way, you can just call me Merry. You may have noticed that we run a somewhat casual office."

"Well, yes, I—"

"Dear Mrs. Benton," Merry began without further preamble, reaching for a creased sheet of paper in front of her and looking at it as she spoke. "In reference to your letter..."

Swallowing what he suspected was a hysterical chuckle, Grant promptly began to scribble in the unique shorthand he'd developed while taking notes in college classes, and had no difficulty keeping up with Merry's dictation. The embarrassingly fatuous grin remained, slanting his nicely shaped mouth into a rakish curve. He suddenly found that he was enjoying himself immensely, and he settled more comfortably into the undersized chair as his mind finally cleared enough for him to realize what had happened to place him in this position.

His older sister, Leida Carmichael owned a temporary-help service. Obviously he'd been mistaken for one of Leida's temporary helpers. What the hell. If getting these letters out by five would make the pretty Merry love him forever, he'd be delighted to accommodate her. It would be the most worthwhile hour and a half he'd ever spent.

During the next hour he found out some very interesting things about Merry. Her last name was James, she was twenty-eight, she wasn't married or otherwise romantically entangled. Grant discovered these fascinating facts by blatantly eavesdroping on the uninhibited conversations that flowed around him between Merry and her brother, Matthew, and fourteen-year-old twin sisters, Melinda and Meaghan. Before the afternoon was over, the young man Grant had encountered earlier reappeared, sans serape. He turned out to a part-time employee of MerryMakers, Louis Webster, a sophomore at Drury College.

Grant learned a few things about the company, as well. Merry was the leader and driving force, although yet another sister, Marsha—their parents had obviously had a sense of humor and a fondness for the letter M—seemed to keep the day-to-day routine running smoothly. Marsha had been bedridden for a week with the flu. Despite the afterschool "help" from her younger sisters and ample advice from Matthew, whom Grant gathered did not work in Merry's business, Merry had called on Leida for assistance on this Wednesday afternoon.

Grant paused for a moment in his letter-typing to wonder why Leida had failed to respond to the request. That wasn't like his superorganized sister. Still, Grant was glad she'd fallen down on the job this once. He was having the time of his life just observing this eccentric family at work. He was also suddenly grateful that the lean, early years of Futron Inc. had meant that he and Tim had both had to learn rudimentary secretarial skills until they'd been able to hire someone to assist them.

He grinned at the typewriter when he realized he was actually having fun. As much as he'd been enjoying his visit with his sister, he'd admitted to himself only that morning that he was beginning to get bored with the vacation he was taking. He'd thrived on work and responsibility for so long that he didn't exactly know how to enjoy such carefree leisure time. He'd spent the past couple of days toying with the idea of starting a new business and wondering if Tim were bored enough with his "beach bunnies" by now to discuss it with him.

Some discreet snooping told Grant that Merry-Makers had been in business for slightly more than a year, that it was operating in the black, though just barely, and that there were more parties on the calendar for the next few months than he supposed the company could have handled. About half the income came from those parties, the other half from the sale and rental of party supplies. He also checked behind a few doors, finding warehouse-type storerooms containing the most fascinating collection of...well, junk that Grant had ever seen. It took little imagination to visualize the party themes available from MerryMakers. Mexican, Hawaiian, Western, Oriental. Themes of the forties, the fifties and the sixties. Tasseled pillows piled under a sheet in one corner of the room made him think of an Arabian fantasy; a roulette wheel and other gambling paraphernalia hinted at casino nights. Other boxes and sheet-covered items indicated that still more themes were available.

"What do you think?" Merry's harmonious voice inquired from behind him as he examined one particularly interesting room.

Grant turned with a smile. "Fascinating. Quite a collection you have here."

His interest obviously pleased her. "Thanks. It's a hectic business, but it's fun."

"Tell me, do you actually attend all the parties you arrange?"

"Most of them. Marsha and I take turns supervising when it's necessary. Other times we're hired only to decorate and clean up afterward, not to actually run the party."

"Isn't there anyone else who works here? Besides the twins and Louis, I mean."

"Oh, sure. We have four part-time workers, including Louis, who set up decorations and work the parties. Marsha and I run the office, and the twins help out after school each afternoon."

"Your parents must be quite proud of their family, running such a successful business," Grant complimented her.

He knew he'd said the wrong thing when her expressive eyes turned suddenly sad. "Our parents are dead, Grant."

"I'm sorry," he murmured. Now he remembered that Melinda had called Merry her legal guardian. He wished he'd stopped to think about that before he'd spoken. He tried to think of something to say to put the smile back in Merry's beautiful eyes, but before he could, she shook off her sadness and gave him that slightly lopsided smile again.

"I'm still thoroughly impressed with you, you know," she confided ingenuously. "I never would have believed you'd have gotten those letters off by a quarter to five. And not a typo in the batch."

"Just doing my job, ma'am," he drawled, pulling at an imaginary forelock of his gold-dusted brown hair in a dramatically subservient manner intended to make her laugh.

It did. Merry's laughter spilled softly over him. He could almost feel it on his skin. He very nearly shivered.

Something must have changed in his eyes because her laughter suddenly died and she looked at him in a kind of wonder. Grant caught his breath at the awareness written on her face. Thank goodness he wasn't the only one affected by this attraction that had hit him so unexpectedly, he thought.

Merry opened her mouth as if to say something, then turned her head when the telephone rang in the reception area behind her. "I'd better get that. The twins left ten minutes ago." She walked into the other room, leaving Grant fully aware that he and Merry were now alone in the offices. Glancing at his watch, he noted that it was fifteen minutes after five. He'd entered the door of this intriguing company over an hour and a half earlier. He would never have believed that he could enjoy that much time playing at secretary for a delightfully unconventional employer. Already choosing the words he would use to invite her to dinner, he followed her into the reception area.

"Leida!" he heard her say. He gulped. *Well, damn.* He wondered what Leida would say when she found out Grant was here. His intentions about canceling the party had changed since he'd met Merry.

Smiling brightly at Grant, Merry continued, "I wanted to tell you—what? A car accident?" She listened for a moment, her eyes narrowing at Grant, then spoke very slowly. "You mean you sent a woman to help me out this afternoon, but she had a car accident and didn't make it? She wasn't hurt, was she? Good. No, don't worry about it, Leida. We managed to get everything done. I'll talk to you tomorrow. Bye."

Merry replaced the receiver very precisely on its cradle, drew in a deep breath, crossed her arms under her breasts and turned to face the man who was smiling so ruefully at her. It wasn't the first time she'd looked at him since he'd arrived, but suddenly she saw him in a different light. Though not overly tall, he was a big man, broad shouldered and solid, with well-defined muscles outlined by his white cotton shirt and dark poplin slacks. Deeply tanned, he sported a firm, almost cleft chin, a very straight nose and a no-nonsense upper lip. He wore his golden-brown hair brushed back from his broad forehead. Though an icy shade of blue, his eyes reflected a surprising amount of warmth; the pupils were ringed with a darker blue and shadowed by short brown lashes. The lids drooped just slightly at the outer edges, giving him a sexy, sleepy look. Who the hell was he?

"Who the hell are you?" she demanded.

The deep creases at the corners of his mouth deepened with his smile. "My name is Grant Bryant." He seemed to find something amusing in his answer.

"You've explained that," Merry said with exaggerated patience. "What are you doing here?"

He slid one hand into his pocket, further stretching the dark fabric of his slacks. Merry kept her eyes trained fiercely on his face. "I'm Leida Carmichael's brother. I came to talk to you about the party you're arranging for her."

Merry felt her cheeks going deep red. "Why didn't you tell me?"

He chuckled. "I never had the chance. Every time I said Leida's name, I was directed to your office. Then you handed me a pad and pencil and started dictating."

"And you just sat there and took the letters." Merry covered her burning cheeks with icy hands. "You typed them and everything."

"It seemed to be expected of me," he explained diffidently.

"Oh, Grant, I'm so sorry," she wailed, dropping her hands. "You must think I'm an idiot. It's just that everything was so hectic, and when you said Leida's name—"

"Hey, don't apologize." He was obviously struggling not to laugh. "I could have explained, but then I realized I was having fun."

"You were having fun taking dictation and typing letters?" she repeated, looking up at him with a frown.

"And watching you," he added, his voice deepening with meaning.

Her cheeks darkened again, despite her efforts to stop feeling so embarrassed. He undoubtedly thought she was an idiot, Merry decided despairingly.

"You owe me for an hour and fifteen minutes' work," Grant informed her suddenly.

She felt a giggle forming in her throat as the humor of the situation finally got to her. "How much?"

"Have dinner with me this evening."

"You work cheap, don't you?" She looked up at him with a smile.

"Actually, I would consider myself very well paid," Grant answered without returning the smile.

Merry caught her breath at the look in his eyes. *Oh, no,* she moaned silently. *Don't do this to me. I don't have time for this.*

"Thank you for the invitation, Grant," she said too breathlessly. "But I can't have dinner with you tonight. Marsha's sick and I have to make dinner for the twins."

Grant thought the twins were quite old enough to make dinner for themselves, but he decided not to argue with her on that point. "Tomorrow night?"

"I have a party tomorrow night."

He knew that. He'd seen the calendar. She had parties booked for the next three nights in a row. He wasn't going to wait that long to see her again. "How long will Marsha be out of commission?"

Eyeing him curiously, she shrugged one shoulder. "The doctor told her to take off at least another few days. She's had a particularly virulent form of flu. Why?"

He grinned broadly. He was sorry for Marsha, of course—well, a little sorry—but Merry's answer couldn't have pleased him more. "Okay, then I'll see you in the morning. You open at nine, don't you?"

"In the morning?" Her frown deepened. "Why? If it has to do with your sister's party, you can tell me now."

"No, it's not that," he assured her airily. "But you still need some office help and I just happen to be available. And, as you pointed out, I work cheap."

"Grant, you can't—"

"Sure I can. No typos, remember?"

She was beginning to understand how he'd felt when he'd entered her office only to be swept into a situation he couldn't control. She was feeling exactly the same way. "No, really, Grant—"

"Come on. I'll walk you to your car. Got everything?"

"Well, yes, but—"

"Fine. Do you live far from here?"

"Would you please let me finish a sentence?" she demanded in amused exasperation.

He leaned over to kiss the end of her nose. "Frustrating, isn't it?" he asked commiseratingly.

Merry could only stare at him, her heart doing flip-flops. He'd kissed her on the nose!

Still grinning, Grant placed a hand on her back and escorted her out the door into the crisp mid-April air. He stood by while she mutely locked up and stayed right by her side as she unlocked the door of her s.nall car. Finally finding her voice, she tried again to reason with him. "Grant, really, you can't work for me."

"Tell you what. If you don't like my work, you can fire me. See you in the morning, boss." He gave her a jaunty wave and spun on his heel, heading cheerfully toward his own vehicle.

A Ferrari, Merry moaned, sinking heavily behind the wheel of her own battered Chevy. Her new temporary secretary was climbing into a red Ferrari. How had this happened, anyway? And what did he want from her? The red Ferrari centered squarely in her rearview mirror, she drove out of the parking lot and turned for home, noting that he drove away in the opposite direction. Only when she was halfway home did it occur to her that he'd never told her what had brought him to Merry-Makers that afternoon, other than that it concerned the party his sister was giving in ten days.

GRANT WHISTLED CHEERILY as he entered his sister's living room a little while later. Leida looked up in surprise. He'd been quite annoyed with her when she'd left for work that morning. That was about the time he'd found out from her teenage son, Chip, that Leida had already made plans to throw a party in Grant's honor, despite his objections.

"Where've you been?" she asked her brother, examining the roguish glint in his eyes.

Grant sauntered across the room to place an arm around his forty-five-year-old sister's plump shoulders. Dropping a kiss on her fair, rouged cheek, he grinned down into the face that bore a definite resemblance to his own, light blue eyes and all. "I paid a visit to Merry-Makers this afternoon."

Leida sighed gustily. "That's why you're so cheerful. You canceled my party, didn't you? Dammit, Grant, I've already invited people. And I'll lose my deposit!"

Grant ruffled her impeccably styled, artfully frosted hair, a gesture he knew perfectly well that she disliked. "Don't worry about it, sis. The party's still on."

"You mean they talked you out of canceling it?"

"The subject never came up," he replied, flopping down on her elegant gold chintz sofa. "Things were kind of hectic around there."

Leida moaned. "I know. I was supposed to send Merry some help, but the woman ran a stop sign and hit a police car, of all the stupid things. And then she didn't have the nerve to call and tell me until it was too late to send a replacement. I'm giving her one more chance to redeem herself with my service, and then I'm going to have to let her go if she doesn't do better. She's a good secretary, but no common sense at all."

"No problem. I gave them a hand at MerryMakers. And don't bother to send anyone tomorrow. I'm going to fill in until Marsha's back on her feet."

Leida's mouth dropped open. "You? Grant, they need someone to do clerical work. That's Marsha's responsibility."

"Yes, I know. I did three letters this afternoon. I noticed the filing has piled up in Marsha's absence. I'll tackle that tomorrow." He thoroughly enjoyed watching the changing expressions on Leida's face. He considered her well served for forcing him to be the guest of honor at one of her parties.

Sudden comprehension illuminated Leida's sharp eyes. "Did you develop this Good Samaritan urge before or after you met Merry James?"

"Actually, it was her idea. The minute I mentioned your name, she poked a pad and pencil at me and started dictating. She thought you'd sent me."

"Grant, you can't do this. You have to tell Merry the truth."

"Oh, she knows I'm your brother. She found out when you called to explain about the woman you'd originally sent. But I smoothed things out and volunteered my services for the remainder of the week."

"And Merry accepted?" Leida asked in bewilderment.

"Well, I really didn't give her much choice," he replied with a decidedly cocky grin.

Leida glared at that grin. "I take it that secretarial skills were not the only, um, service you offered?"

"Let's just say they're the only ones she accepted . . . for now."

Leida dropped wearily into an armchair and rubbed her temples. "I can't believe this is my rational, usually sane brother that I'm talking to. Grant, I've never known you to go to such lengths just to set up a fling with a pretty brunette. For that matter, I've never known you to indulge in that many flings."

Grant scowled at her candid evaluation of his past love life. "I'm not anticipating a vacation fling with Merry James, Leida. She's not the type."

"So what are you telling me?" she demanded suspiciously. She smiled weakly, attempting a lighter tone.

"That you've fallen desperately in love with her and are planning wedding bells and orange blossoms?"

Grant pushed himself to his feet and stood smiling down at her. "You always did know me very well, sister, dear."

Leida groaned and covered her face with her hands. "You're doing it again, aren't you?"

"Doing what?"

"You've found something you want and you're going to go after it full throttle. Even though this 'something' is a human being with a mind of her own. I'm warning you, Grant, Merry may not appreciate being hustled by a single-minded male."

He only grinned and turned to leave the room. At the doorway he stopped and looked over his shoulder at her. "Be sure and invite Tim to your party, will you? I want him to meet Merry."

"Grant!" Leida yelled after him, but too late. He was gone, whistling again as he walked briskly down the hallway.

Grant headed straight for the shower, pulling at the buttons of his white shirt as the besotted smile remained fixed on his bronze face. He was actually looking forward to Leida's party, he realized with some amusement. He only hoped the tasseled satin pillows were not a part of the decorations his sister had ordered.

2

"WHAT A FOX!" Meaghan's voice oozed with adolescent awe.

"Oh, Marsha, you should have seen him. Golden-brown hair, piercing blue eyes. And that body!" Melinda sighed gustily, her green eyes dreamy.

"Well, Merry?" Marsha inquired, her voice husky from her raw throat. "Are they exaggerating?"

Merry concentrated on the chicken casserole on the plate in front of her. "No, they're not exaggerating. He's very good-looking."

"You were late getting home tonight," Melinda commented, eyeing her eldest sister with a quizzically lifted eyebrow. "Were you by any chance rating the new employee's, um, performance?"

"Melinda James!" Merry gasped as both the twins dissolved into giggles and Marsha smiled into the chicken broth she was trying to choke down. "Eat your dinner," Merry added sternly, the glare she turned on her younger sister mitigated by the sparkle in her green eyes.

"You have to admit it was amusing," Marsha croaked. "Not Melinda's comment," she clarified with a pseudo-scowl at the twin in question. "The mix-up in identity. Poor Grant must have been thoroughly bewildered when he found himself suddenly taking dictation."

With a low moan Merry covered her cheeks in remembered embarrassment. "I know. I felt like such a fool when I found out what I'd done."

"A red Ferrari," irrepressible Melinda sighed. "A hunk in a red Ferrari. Oh, why couldn't I be a few years older?"

"Then you'd be competing with Merry," Meaghan, usually the quieter of the twins, pointed out mischievously. "You might not have noticed the way the guy was looking at her, but I sure did. Besides, you're only interested in Savage, aren't you?"

"You're right," Melinda acknowledged cheerfully. "Hey, Merry, think Grant will loan me the Ferrari when he's my brother-in-law?"

"Not on your life," Merry answered without thinking. Then, when the others laughed, she shook her head vigorously and glared around the table. "I mean, there's no chance that he'll be your brother-in-law. Would you be serious? I just met the guy and I hardly made a wonderful first impression."

"He looked pretty impressed to me," Meaghan retorted bravely. "Every time you bent over the file cabinet, I thought he was going to hyperventilate."

"And you turned down a date with him," Melinda accused Merry in patent disgust. "I can't believe it. Real smart move."

Merry quickly changed the subject, mentioning to Marsha that their brother, Matt, had dropped in at the office earlier.

"He's really giving me a pain, Merry," Melinda complained. "Can't you talk to him? Geez, ever since he turned twenty-five and got that promotion at work, you'd think he was God. Thinks he knows it all."

"He told me that I had on too much makeup today." Meaghan patted her peach-enhanced cheeks with scarlet fingertips. "Can you believe it? Like he was my father or something."

"And he yelled at me for bringing home a C in math," Melinda added resentfully. "Why'd you have to tell him, Merry? I told you I'd bring the grade up next time."

Merry sighed. "All right, I'll talk to him," she promised. "Give him a break, will you? Matt's only trying to help out. He feels responsible for you. For all of us, really. He thinks he's helping me by trying to keep an eye on you."

"Well, he's not the eldest. You are. And I'd rather have you for a guardian than him anytime," Melinda stated defiantly. "And I won't stop seeing Savage, no matter what Matthew says."

Marsha pushed aside the chicken broth she'd barely touched. "Merry said she would talk to him for you," she pointed out, looking at both teenagers as she spoke softly. "And she's right. Matt is only trying to help. So ease up, will you? Merry's tired." She cleared her throat. "Since everyone seems to be finished with dinner, you can start cleaning up now."

Merry and Marsha usually cooked the meals, and the twins cleaned up afterward. Sighing, they followed Marsha's instructions, identical looks of resignation on their identical faces. Merry thought vaguely that she really should talk to the twins about changing their appearance a bit to make them more individual. They'd been dressing exactly alike since birth and continued to do so from habit. Though reluctant to criticize her mother's decisions on child-raising, Merry wondered if it would be healthier for the twins to be more distinguishable in their appearance. Then she turned her thoughts back to her other sister.

"You need to get back to bed," she told Marsha, eyeing her sister's pale cheeks. Her bout with the flu had left purple shadows under her large gray eyes—Marsha was

the only one of the James siblings who had her father's
gray eyes rather than her mother's green ones—and her
Cupid's bow mouth pale in her white face. Her silvery-
blond hair was held back with a ribbon rather than
bouncing around her shoulders in her usual style.

Not until they were alone in Marsha's room later did
Grant's name come up again. Merry hadn't consciously
gone into Marsha's room to discuss Grant, but she was
aware that she gave the appearance that something was
on her mind. Without looking at her sister Merry moved
around restlessly, rearranging the items on the nightstand, straightening the shade on the bedside lamp.

Watching closely from where she reclined against her
pillows, Marsha asked, "Is something wrong?"

Merry quickly turned her head. "No, of course not.
Why do you ask?"

Rather than giving a direct answer, Marsha tried another question. "Why did you turn down Grant's invitation to dinner? He sounds very nice."

"Well, yes, he is nice," Merry responded warily,
perching on the edge of Marsha's bed. "I mean, I think
he is. After all, I hardly know him."

"But he's Leida's brother, and you've known her for
years."

"I couldn't go out with him tonight," Merry repeated
firmly. "You're ill and the kids had to eat."

"As Melinda pointed out to you earlier, we *can* take
care of ourselves," Marsha reminded her older sister with
gentle humor. "Especially for a few hours. So what's the
real reason you turned him down, Merry?"

Merry exhaled and looked down at her fingers as she
twisted them in her lap. "He made me nervous," she admitted.

"In what way?" Marsha prodded, suddenly concerned. "Did he do anything—"

"Oh, no, he was a perfect gentleman," Merry broke in quickly. "Really a good sport about everything. I'm sure his dinner invitation was quite respectable."

"So how did he make you nervous?"

Merry pictured the look in Grant's eyes when he'd asked her out. That intense, sexy, speculative look that had let her know he found her attractive. Desirable. She'd admitted to herself then that she found him equally desirable. The admission had unnerved her. It had been so long since...well, since anyone had made her feel quite that way. "He's so good-looking," she mused aloud. "And when he smiles at me, my mind goes completely blank. I think maybe...I think he's interested in me," she confessed modestly.

"And what's wrong with that?" Marsha demanded, struggling with a smile.

"Marsha, I don't have the time to get involved with anyone right now. You know that. The business is just starting to turn a profit and it involves so many long hours. Then there's the family. With the twins so active in extracurricular activities, someone's always having to be chauffeured somewhere. I have laundry to do and books to balance and—"

Marsha laughed. "Honestly, Merry. The man only asked you out to dinner. He didn't offer a full-scale love affair."

Merry's cheeks burned. "I know that," she muttered.

"And what if it *did* turn into something more serious?" Marsha continued, warming to her subject. "Would that be so bad? You're twenty-eight, Merry James, and though you go out often enough, you haven't been seriously involved with anyone since Justin Spencer. That's been five years."

"You know why Justin and I broke up."

"Yes, I know." They shared a solemn silence as both thought back to that terrible time five years earlier when their parents had been killed in a boating accident. As the eldest at twenty-three, Merry had immediately assumed responsibility for her grief-stricken younger brother and sisters. Her finacé, Justin, only twenty-six himself, had not been willing to share that responsibility. Merry had loved him very much, and his defection on top of her own grief had been devastating. But she had allowed herself little time to give in to self-pity as she'd taken over the support of her family, budgeting insurance money, the school-age children's social security benefits and her own salary to pay bills and tuitions until she'd been able to start her own business.

She'd stayed very busy. Staying very busy had eventually become a habit.

Marsha roused herself to lecture Merry again. "Justin was self-centered and immature. You've stayed away from serious relationships since him because you think all men are like him. They're not, Merry."

"Perhaps not." Merry sighed. "But I haven't met one lately who was interested in taking on the responsibility of two teenagers. Or who was willing to acknowledge that our business is a serious commitment, as much as any business, and that it takes time to make it successful. Most men act as if just because we give parties for a living, we should be able to take off anytime we like for fun and games with them. Remember how irritated Joe Borden was when I turned down his invitation to that fund-raiser because we had that huge party in Joplin scheduled that night? It's different when *he* has to work late, because *he's* a tax accountant and that's so much more important than our little theme parties." Her lip curled in disgust.

Marsha giggled. "I certainly didn't mean to get you onto your soapbox! I know men don't always make allowances for women's careers, but I'll say again, not all men are like that."

Taking a deep breath, Merry jumped to her feet and straightened the bedspread where she'd been sitting. "Look, Marsha, there's no need to go into this tonight. As you said, Grant only asked me for dinner."

"And you refused because he's the first man in five years who really turns you on." Marsha squirmed discontentedly beneath her frilly bedspread.

"Why don't you watch some TV?" Merry suggested, handing her sister the remote control to a small color set at the foot of the bed. "There's a good movie starting in a few minutes, isn't there? You said you wanted to see it."

"Just think about what I said, will you, Merry?"

"I'll think about it," Merry promised. "Call me if you need anything, Marsha. I'm going to work on the books for a while."

MERRY DROPPED HER PURSE into a desk drawer and seated herself. Nine o'clock. MerryMakers was open for business on this routine Thursday morning. And Grant Bryant was conspicuously absent.

"I knew he was only teasing," she muttered. She pushed aside a folded copy of the *Springfield News-Leader* with its prominent headline of a sudden rash of burglaries in the area, and pulled her appointment calendar in front of her. Grant had amused himself for an hour or so with her, but he hadn't really planned to show up this morning. She wasn't sure if she was relieved or disappointed. "You're relieved, Merry," she told herself aloud. She glanced at the desk in front of her, piled with work waiting for her attention. "You don't have time for foolishness."

And an involvement of any type with Grant Bryant, no matter how brief, would definitely be foolish, she added sternly. The man was dangerous. No man before him—not even Justin—had been able to turn her into a quivering lunatic with only a smile. It was a terribly uncomfortable feeling.

The offices were so quiet with no one there but Merry. Usually this was the time of day when she and Marsha got the most work done, before the client calls normally began, while the twins were in school. Merry missed having Marsha around to talk to. And, besides that, there was so much to be done. She drew a deep breath and picked up her pen.

She'd left the door to her office open as usual, so when she heard someone enter the outer office a short while later, she looked up curiously. The pen fell from her fingers with a small clatter. Grant Bryant had returned.

"I know, I'm thirty minutes late," he began apologetically, straightening his striped tie as he combed his windblown hair with his fingers. "Inexcusable for my first day, isn't it? I'm afraid I forgot to set my alarm."

Merry resisted the impulse to press a hand to her thudding heart. "Grant . . ."

"Oldest excuse in the book, right?" he asked with an exaggerated sigh. "Sorry. You'll just have to dock me for half an hour. Now what shall I tackle first? Filing? Letters? Any special typing you need done?"

"Grant, you can't do this."

"Of course I can," he returned, looking offended. "I'm very good in an office."

Merry rose to her feet. *"Why* are you doing this?" she demanded.

Grant leaned against her doorjamb and smiled at her. She looked even better than he'd remembered, he decided. And that was saying a lot. The crisp green shirt-dress she wore exactly matched her eyes and, in combination with that dark brown hair swaying at her shoulders, made him think again of chocolate mint. It was rapidly becoming his favorite flavor. He wondered if she would taste minty fresh if he were to grab her and kiss her silly.

"Grant," Merry repeated impatiently as he only looked at her with that smile that went straight to her hormones, "I asked you a question. Why are you doing this?"

He pushed himself away from the doorway and walked slowly toward her. It was no use trying to be noble and gentlemanly at this moment, he reflected. He simply had to taste her.

Merry felt her eyes going wide as she stared up at him. "What are you doing?" she asked huskily, reading the intention in his face.

"I'm going to kiss you," he replied evenly, stopping only inches away from her.

"You . . ." She swallowed. "You are?"

"Yep." His hands fell gently on her shoulders. "I am."

"Oh." She wondered if she should bother to demur when she had no intention of stopping him. She had wanted to know what his kiss would be like ever since he'd dropped that unexpected little peck onto her nose the day before. Still, the man was practically a stranger. Perhaps she should . . .

He gave her no opportunity to do anything but cooperate. His mouth settled on hers gently, but firmly, even as his hands moved from her shoulder to gather her close to him.

Merry told herself later that her hands had gone up and around his neck only to push him away. Of course she hadn't intended for the kiss to turn into the most thorough, most explosive embrace in her experience.

Grant took full advantage of her weakness. Lifting her onto her toes to hold her even closer against him, he swept the moist depths of her mouth with his tongue. Her arms tightened around his neck reflexively, and he almost moaned as the movement pressed her small, firm breasts more snugly against his chest. He wanted to touch her, to explore every inch of her compact, pulsing body, to strip away the mint-green dress and bury himself in the warmth and softness of her. He'd known desire, but never before had he felt this all-consuming hunger. He'd enjoyed physical union, but he had never considered that joining necessary to make him complete.

Whether because he was shaken by the unprecedented emotions sweeping through him or because he'd suddenly become aware of the awkwardness of making love in her office during business hours, Grant forced himself to draw back from her. His entire body protested the action. Taking a deep, steadying breath, he brought his arms from around her until only his hands were holding her, resting unsteadily on her shoulders.

Merry's eyes were glazed, her face flushed. Her mouth trembled, still moist from his, and he almost forgot all consequences and grabbed her again. Some previously unknown source of strength within him allowed him to smile, albeit weakly, and speak in a relatively normal tone. "Shall I make some coffee before I tackle the filing?"

Coffee? Merry blinked, trying to remember if she'd ever heard the word before.

"Merry?"

Her name on Grant's lips, spoken with husky undertones of indulgent amusement, brought her out of her trance. She blinked and pressed her hands to her burning cheeks. "Oh. I, uh, the coffee's already made."

"Great. I could use a cup. I'll get you one, too. Do you take anything in it?"

"A little sugar." She shook her head slowly to clear away the last vestiges of bemusement. *This is ridiculous*, she told herself in annoyance. How could she let one kiss do this to her?

"Grant." She tried to speak forcefully, but even she heard the slight quaver in her voice.

He paused when he would have moved away. "Yes?"

"Why are you here?" she asked again.

He reached out to trace her lower lip with one blunt forefinger. "Because I couldn't stay away," he answered simply. Then he walked away from her to pour them both some coffee before starting the filing.

Merry sat behind her desk, her perfectly sweetened coffee cooling at her elbow as she tried very hard to concentrate on her work. But how could she concentrate on order sheets and numbers when her entire body still quivered with the feelings Grant had aroused in her? Her gaze drifted toward the reception area, where Grant hummed softly as he rapidly reduced the stack of filing that she'd been piling on Marsha's desk for the past week.

For at least the hundredth time in the past twenty minutes she heard his deep voice speaking the words that had robbed her of logical thought ever since. *"Because I couldn't stay away,"* he had told her.

What had he meant by that? Could he really be feeling the same emotions that were swirling inside her? Attraction, desire, hunger, need?

Impossible. She wasn't the type to bring out those emotions in a man she'd known such a short time. She was too wholesome, too small. No sex goddess, though Grant certainly had a way of making her feel sexy and desirable. Something about the way he looked at her . . .

She really should ask him to leave. But, dammit, she liked having him here. Her hand clenched into a fist on her desk. *Oh, Merry, you are such a fool.*

When the telephone buzzed, she snatched up the receiver eagerly, punching the flashing button with a snap. She desperately needed a distraction from the man behind her sister's desk. A distraction from her own dangerous thoughts.

"MerryMakers."

"Merry? Hi, it's Leida. Is my pesky little brother there bugging you again?"

Merry managed to smile at Leida's inappropriate description of Grant. "As a matter of fact, he is. Do you want to talk to him?"

"No. I may never talk to him again. I'm really sorry, hon. I don't know what's gotten into him. He's been unemployed for less than three weeks and already he's into mischief. I should have known this would happen."

Unemployed? Merry was startled but managed not to ask questions. Leida sounded as if she thought Merry were aware of that fact, as if Grant should have told her.

"But I guess you know all about troublesome little brothers, don't you, Merry?" Leida continued humorously.

"I guess so," Merry answered uncertainly. She had a hard time picturing Grant as anyone's troublesome little brother.

"Of course you do. Anyway, I called to see if you need me to send someone around today. I doubt that you'll want Grant messing around in your office all day."

She really should take Leida up on the offer, Merry told herself. All she had to do was to tell Grant that help was on the way and that he would have to leave and allow her to get on with her business. She looked back toward the reception area just as he looked around at her. Their eyes met and held. "No, thanks, Leida, I don't need anyone today. Everything's under control right now, and the twins will be in to help after school," Merry heard herself saying.

"Well, okay, if you're sure. Call me if you need anyone next week."

"Yes, I will."

"Good. I'll let you go now. I'm sure you've got your hands full."

Merry wondered what Leida meant by that but chose not to ask.

"I take it Leida's checking up on me?" Grant asked from the doorway as Merry hung up the phone.

"Yes, that was Leida. She wanted to know if you were still bugging me."

He grinned, crossing his arms over his broad chest. "I suppose you said yes."

"Of course. She also asked if I wanted her to send someone over to help out this afternoon."

Grant frowned. "What did you tell her?"

"I told her no," Merry admitted with a sigh of frustration.

He smiled again. "Good."

"Only because I really didn't need anyone," Merry hastened to explain to him.

"Of course not. You've got me."

"That's not what I meant," she muttered.

"I know. By the way, when's lunch?"

"Lunch?" she repeated incredulously, looking at her watch. "Grant, it's ten-fifteen."

"Just like to be prepared," he replied imperturbably. "I want to take you somewhere really nice."

"Now wait a minute. I never said I'd have lunch with you."

"You never said you wouldn't, either," he pointed out.

"That's because you didn't ask!"

"Right. I find that I avoid a lot of rejection that way." Before she could answer that particularly audacious comment, he turned back toward the filing cabinets. "Excuse me. I have work to do," he told her gravely.

Merry drew in a deep breath, but before she could lambaste him, the telephone rang again. "I'll get that!" she almost yelled when she saw his hand reaching for the phone on the reception desk.

Grant only shrugged, smiled and picked up another stack of folders.

Merry concluded the business call with surprising professionalism, considering the way her mind was spinning, then hung up and stared soberly into her cold coffee.

She could not afford to become involved with this man, she told herself flatly.

Unfortunately, she was afraid that she already was involved.

"MERRY, YOU'RE GOING to break your neck."

"Don't worry about it, Grant. I do this all the time."

"Not in front of me you don't. Get down. I'll finish that."

"Grant, would you let me do my job? Find something else to do, if you want to be helpful." Perched on the very top step of a tall wooden ladder, the jeans and sneakers she'd changed into at the office providing a suitable uniform for this other facet of her career, she glared down at the man looking up at her in concern. A dangling mobile of 45 records strung on fishing line hung from her right hand, ready to be stapled to a rafter just above her head.

Grant turned his head and caught Melinda's eye as she walked past him. He knew it was Melinda because Meaghan was home studying for a test while the rest of the crew decorated a local country club for the sock hop MerryMakers was coordinating that evening. "Melinda, take these, please," he said, dumping the stack of posters he'd just brought in from the truck into the teenager's willing arms.

"Sure, Grant." Melinda balanced the rolled posters and stood back with a grin, waiting for the outcome of the battle of wills between her stubborn sister and the intriguing man who seemed to have joined their staff that day.

Grant placed firm hands on the ladder to steady it, then looked back up at Merry. "Down," he ordered her. "Now."

Merry tossed her head. "Go away. I'm busy." She reached above her head with the hand holding the mobile, her other clutching the staple gun. Chagrined, she felt herself wobble a bit as the movement threatened her precarious balance. Since she had performed this particular operation hundreds of times in the past without incident, she attributed her uncharacteristic unsteadiness

to the fact that Grant was hanging around beneath her,
waiting for her to fall.

"Dammit, Merry, come down off that ladder, or I'm
coming up after you!" Grant roared, his hands tightening on the ladder as she swayed.

Furious, she started to tell him exactly what he could
do with his order. And then she noticed that everyone in
the room had stopped what they were doing to watch the
confrontation between the "boss" and the man that
everyone thought was temporary office help. Since
"everyone" included Melinda, Louis and Mrs. Devore,
the president of Business and Professional Women—the
organization sponsoring the sock hop—Merry knew that
she was going to have to extricate herself from this embarrassing situation with as much dignity as possible.
The oath she muttered between clenched teeth would
have earned the twins a severe scolding.

She set the staple gun on the top of the ladder and
looked down at Grant. "Catch," she told him, dropping
the mobile in his direction. Irritated by the scene he was
making, she found herself hoping he would fumble the
mobile and stop looking so smug.

But Grant was quick. He caught the cascade of records easily and set them in a pile at his feet before grasp-
ing the ladder again. "Watch your step coming down,"
he said with grave courtesy.

Seething, she climbed gracefully down the ladder and
stepped away, waving a hand to indicate that Grant was
welcome to take her place. "It's all yours," she told him.
And I hope you break both your legs, her sparkling green
eyes added.

He grinned ferally, obviously well aware of her sub-
liminal message. "Yes, boss," he returned mockingly, and

scooped up the mobile before ascending the sturdy ladder.

Merry turned her back on him, supremely indifferent to his safety, then gasped and whirled around when she heard his foot slip. Catching himself immediately, he tossed her a cocky smile and continued upward, undoubtedly knowing that he'd just caused her heart to stop.

"Come on, Melinda. Let's get these posters up," Merry said brusquely.

"Yes, boss," Melinda drawled, imitating Grant.

This has been the longest day of my life, Merry fumed as she fixed a James Dean poster to the wall with circles of masking tape. Grant had taken over her entire day since showing up at her office at nine-thirty. He had worked steadily all morning, stopping only to take her to lunch at her favorite seafood restaurant. When Louis and Melinda had arrived in the afternoon, they'd loaded the delivery van with decorations for the party and, leaving another part-time employee to answer the office telephones, had come to the country club to set up. Merry had told Grant that he needn't come along, but of course he had ignored her—just as he'd been ignoring similar hints all day.

The worst part was that Grant had lost no opportunity to flirt with her or touch her, though—thank God—he had not repeated that incredible kiss. It was becoming harder and harder for Merry to remember that she could not possibly become involved with him. Every time he came near her, her heart started pounding and her kneecaps turned to oatmeal.

Torn between her unwanted attraction to him and her indignation with his high-handedness, she tilted a poster of Marilyn Monroe at a provocative angle and attached it to the wall near James Dean.

"This place looks great. You really go all out, don't you?" Grant's voice, so close to her ear, made her jump and drop the poster of Bogart and Bacall that she'd planned to tape up next. He smiled down at her, pleased that his proximity seemed to make her uncomfortable. Her closeness sure as hell made *him* uncomfortable.

Merry retrieved the poster and glanced up at him through her lashes. "I like to give the customers their money's worth."

"Well, you've done that here," he told her with warm approval, looking around the room. Hula hoops and records hung from the ceiling, pom-poms decorated various corners and tables, crepe paper and balloons had been liberally utilized, and a streamer-laden basketball goal had been hung above a white-draped bandstand. They'd set up a reproduction of an old soda fountain in one corner, complete with chrome-and-pink vinyl stools. In another corner a photographer's station had been set up, decorated in theme, for those guests who wanted a clever memento of the evening. The huge posters of the 1950s stars added to the authentic setting of the theme. "I feel like I've stepped into one of Leida's yearbooks."

"You mean you don't remember parties like this?" Merry inquired innocently.

Grant grimaced at her. "Give me a break. I'm only thirty-four. Now if you want to talk about the sixties..."

Smiling, she shook her head. "Sorry. The seventies were more my time."

"So how did you manage to make this look so authentic?" he asked. Not that he really cared; he just wanted to keep her talking, he decided. He'd caught her off guard with his compliments of her decorating, and now she was smiling at him without the wariness that she deliberately kept between them whenever she remembered. He wished he knew why she felt it necessary to keep barriers between them. He fully intended to find out.

"You said it yourself. I looked through lots of yearbooks from the '50s. Nostalgia's in, so I decided to keep everything as realistic as possible. I haunt flea markets and antique stores for props. It's fun."

Grant reached out to trace her lower lip with one finger; his touch sent her heart into convulsive spasms. "You have the most beautiful smile I've ever seen, boss lady."

Merry's smile faded abruptly. "Excuse me, Grant, Mrs. Devore is motioning for me," she murmured, knowing full well he could tell he'd flustered her, but she was unable to do anything about it. She could feel his laughing eyes focused on her back as she all but scurried away.

3

AS MERRY SOOTHED the preparty jitters of the woman who was responsible for the evening's activities, she continued to watch Grant, her gaze returning to him again and again despite her efforts to control it. He was working at the bandstand with Melinda, talking softly with her as he worked. Melinda was obviously en thralled by him. And so was she, Merry thought with a resigned sigh. She watched him tug teasingly at Melin da's banana-clipped ponytail and scolded herself si lently for feeling jealous of her fourteen-year-old sister.

Before Mrs. Devore could notice that Merry's atten tion had completely drifted away from their conversa tion, a deep voice bellowed out from the doorway, close to where Merry and Mrs. Devore stood. "Hey, yo! Mel inda! Over here!"

Merry's gaze turned, as did everyone else's, to stare at the glowering young man in the doorway. He looked completely out of place in the tastefully elegant country club with its frivolous decorations—but then, Savage tended to look out of place wherever he happened to be, Merry acknowledged ruefully. Nearing eighteen, Sav age Taylor—whose real first name Merry had yet to learn—wore his brown and bleached-blond hair in a ragged series of layers to his shoulders, had been known to outline his defiant brown eyes with black eyeliner and sported two silver earrings dangling from his left ear and a diamond stud on his right. He refused to be predictable in his choice of clothing; Merry had seen him dressed in anything from skid-road chic to Brooks Brothers prep. Today he was garbed in an oversize black sweater over an untucked red shirt with baggy yellow pants tucked into short black boots.

At her boyfriend's gruff summons Melinda left the bandstand and hurried across the room. "Hi, Savage," she greeted in the besottedly breathless voice she always used with him. "You're a little early picking me up."

"Yeah, whatever," Savage muttered, unconcerned with time. "Who's that guy that was hanging all over you over there?" he demanded audibly, jealousy tinging his rough voice.

Merry grinned, resisting an impulse to shoot a mocking glance at Grant, but the grin faded immediately when Melinda answered with indignant innocence, "Come off it, Savage. That's Grant. He's Merry's."

Merry closed her eyes in embarrassment, having no difficulty avoiding looking toward Grant this time. She knew it was too much to hope that Grant had not heard the clear young voice.

Savage frowned a little, looked from Merry to Grant, then nodded. "Yeah, okay. How you doing, Merry?" he asked, raising his voice slightly, though she stood only six feet away from him.

"Fine, Savage," Merry managed politely. "And you?"

"Yeah," he returned obscurely. "Okay if Melinda takes off now?"

"Yes. Don't forget—"

"She'll be home by ten," Savage broke in to promise, his smile unexpectedly charming. "Just like always."

Merry smiled back at him. Although Matt objected to Savage's punk appearance and occasionally troubled past, Merry had always liked the young man. Savage seemed genuinely fond of Melinda and had given Merry no reason thus far to worry about her younger sister's relationship with him. Which was a great relief since Melinda adored the ground Savage stomped upon. To object to her seeing him would have been an exercise in futility.

"So that's the guy Melinda's dating?" Grant asked Merry a few minutes later, his tone sounding a lot like Matt's at that moment.

Merry nodded. "Yes. Despite his rather eccentric appearance, Savage is really quite nice."

Grant thought of the heated argument he had interrupted between Melinda and Matt, remembering that Matt had objected to the young man's age as well as his appearance. Grant didn't usually judge people like Savage on appearance, but Melinda *was* awfully young... and had such a sweetly innocent smile. "You really think she's old enough to date?" he asked tentatively.

"They're only going for pizza and a movie with some of their friends. A movie I've seen and found completely suitable," Merry returned, her tone reminding him that this was not really his business.

"That boy looks pretty tough. And he's older than Melinda, isn't he?" Grant knew he was treading on shaky ground but couldn't resist making one more comment. For some reason he was concerned about Melinda. He genuinely liked Merry's bubbly little sister.

"Look, Grant," Merry stated flatly. "I can allow Melinda to see Savage, with certain restrictions, or I can forbid her to see him. Doing that would drive a wedge between us and would only mean that she'd sneak around behind my back and see him, anyway. I would intercede if I thought there was any real danger in her dating Savage, but I don't, so stay out of it. The decision is entirely mine."

Grant knew when it was time to back down. "You're right, of course."

"Yes," she agreed. "Now if you'll excuse me, I have to finish up here and then go home to dress for this evening."

"Does your crew dress in theme?" Grant asked her, smiling to erase the slight tension their brief conflict had created.

"Yes, we do." She refused to return the smile. "Grant, there's no reason for you to work tonight. I have all the help I need." She intended to be quite firm about that. The last thing she needed was for Grant to distract her during the party, which would affect her work.

She was rather surprised when he gave in without even a token argument. "Okay. Anything else we need to do here?"

"No, that's all. You and Louis can take the van back to the office now." Merry had driven her own car to the country club, following Grant and Louis who rode in the van.

"Yes, ma'am," Grant responded. "See you later, boss." He tossed her a cocky grin and spun on his heel.

She hated it when he called her "boss," Merry thought, glaring momentarily at his broad back before turning away to find Mrs. Devore.

HE CAME TO THE PARTY, of course. Not as a worker, but as a guest. Merry hadn't realized Leida was a member of Business and Professional Women. Grant came as his sister's escort, giving Merry an unforgivably smug grin when he entered and caught her eye.

"You look cute in your ponytail and teenybopper clothes," Grant drawled a short time later, catching Merry by the refreshment table where she was checking to see if anything needed to be replenished. She'd changed into costume since he'd last seen her—a white cashmere sweater set, a full-circle gray flannel skirt appliquéd with the poodle design so popular in the fifties, turned-down white socks and saddle oxfords. Having just sent Kirk, another college student who worked part-time for her and the only other MerryMakers employee working the sock hop, into the kitchen for more chips, she'd been alone when Grant cornered her.

She glared at Grant, refusing to admit to him that he was breathtakingly attractive in his muscle-molding black T-shirt and faded jeans turned up at the ankles to reveal white socks and scuffed Loafers. He'd even slicked his golden-brown hair back into a modified DA, emphasizing the high temples that Merry found devastatingly sexy. "Why didn't you tell me you were going to be here tonight?"

"I wanted to surprise you," he replied, toying with her ponytail. "Did I?"

"You're past the point of surprising me with anything you do Grant Bryant."

His light blue eyes sparked with mischief and laughter. "You think so?"

She would not get caught in *that* discussion, Merry decided firmly. "I should have realized Leida was a member of BPW," she said, abruptly changing the subject.

"It's a good organization. How come you're not a member?"

"I don't have time," she answered simply. And that completely honest answer reminded her of everything else she didn't have time for—all having to do with Grant.

"Darling, don't you ever do anything just because it might be interesting?"

"Of course I do," she answered crossly. "And don't call me darling." Sheer perversity made her decide not to tell him about the music classes she was taking—just because they were interesting.

"All right, my love, I won't call you darling."

She glared at him. "I'm not your love, either. Honestly, Grant, we've only known each other for a day."

"We have known each other," he informed her, "for twenty-eight hours and—" he checked his watch "—thirty-two minutes, give or take two minutes. That's plenty of time."

"Plenty of time for what?" she asked suspiciously.

"For us to realize that we're perfect for each other, of course." He tugged her ponytail again as he answered cheerfully.

"You," she told him loftily, "are not perfect for me. You're too pushy."

"Assertive," he corrected her, undaunted. "Assertiveness is a highly valued trait in the business world."

She frowned. "Just what is it that you do in the business world, Grant? You've never said."

"I'm between jobs. Are you interested in hiring me fulltime?"

"No."

He winced good-naturedly. "That's honest enough. But I suppose it's for the best. I don't think business and romance mix very well."

"Romance?" she repeated. "There is no romance between us, Grant Bryant."

He smiled meltingly and touched his lips to her forehead. "You're wrong, love. You make me feel very romantic. For the first time in my life, actually."

Desperately in need of a change of subject, and a more manageable distance between herself and this infuriating but oh-so-intriguing man, Merry looked quickly around the crowded colorful room, spotting sandy-haired Kirk headed their way with another batch of chips. She seized on the first excuse that came to mind.

"Excuse me, Grant, I have to see if the Coke box needs refilling." An old, red Coke box had been filled with ice and classic six-ounce Cokes and Nehi grape drinks. A laughing crowd stood around the box, helping themselves to the soft drinks, as well as the hot dogs, chips, pretzels and other snacks displayed on white-paper-and-streamer-adorned tables.

Grant allowed her to walk away, but she knew his gaze never left her. He might as well have walked with her, actually touching her, she told herself with a rueful grimace. She would have been no more aware of him.

Watching her as closely as she suspected, Grant shook his head in regret. Merry was definitely letting her responsibilities to her work and to her family interfere with her personal life. He would like to sit down and point out how badly she was cheating herself by letting her youth pass by in a blur of work and duty. He'd been there. Yet he knew that she would probably not listen to him or take his advice now—just as he probably would not have done some ten years before. Now he could look back and see all that he had missed in his single-minded drive to put Futron on top. Now he knew that he probably could have accomplished the same things without going to the extremes that he had. Merry could make time for herself without sacrificing her business or her family. So how could he convince her of that? He leaned against a poster of Elvis Presley, fingertips in the pockets of his skintight jeans as he contemplated the question.

"LOST HIS MIND. The man has gone around the bend."

Leida's muttering brought Merry's attention from the inside of the half-empty Coke box. She closed the lid and turned to face Grant's sister. Leida looked younger than her forty-five years in her tight-bodiced, bouffant-skirted pink dress, a tiny pink bow clipped into her teased hair, a string of pearls around her throat, short white gloves covering her small hands and low-heeled white pumps on her feet. "I assume you're referring to Grant?" Merry asked with a faint smile.

"Who else?" Leida replied with a heavy sigh. "I haven't seen him act this way since he had a massive crush on Trixie Parker in the seventh grade. Next thing you know, he'll be carving your initials into a tree."

Merry felt her cheeks going crimson. "Oh, I don't think . . ."

Leida only laughed, her light blue eyes twinkling in a manner reminiscent of her younger brother's.

"Leida, I'm sure your brother is very nice," Merry began tactfully, "but I just met him. There's certainly nothing between us."

"I wondered how he would react once he had all the responsibility of that company off his shoulders," Leida murmured as if Merry hadn't spoken. "It's nice to see him concentrating on something besides business for a change."

"What company?" Merry couldn't resist asking.

"Why, *his* company," Leida replied in mild surprise. "Didn't he tell you?"

Merry shook her head.

"Grant and Tim—his best friend and business partner—just sold a company they'd built from scratch right out of college. Those guys put everything they had into that company for the past thirteen years, barely taking time to eat or sleep. There've been times when I've worried about their health. I'll tell you, I was glad when they decided to sell. Though Lord knows what they'll do now. Tim's lounging on a beach somewhere and swears he'll never work another day, though I know better. And Grant . . . well, he—"

"I know what Grant's doing," Merry interrupted. "At least for the past two days."

Leida shrugged and smiled. "Obviously Grant's decided he's got time for a new lady in his life."

Unfortunately, the "new lady" did not have time for Grant, Merry thought glumly when Leida had obeyed a summons from someone across the room. She was relieved to discover that Grant wasn't the irresponsible, unemployed playboy she'd begun to suspect him of being, but this new information did not change her determination to stay out of an involvement with him. Quite the opposite, in fact. Grant had just rid himself of overwhelming responsibilities. He certainly didn't need to begin a relationship with a woman who was responsible for a thriving, demanding business, as well as two teenage siblings. Obviously he had not taken a good look at Merry's situation.

Or, she thought suddenly, perhaps he had no intention of beginning a relationship with her. Could it be that he was pursuing her only out of boredom? Maybe all he had in mind was a brief affair, a fling. Dumb of her not to think of that before, she thought, smoothing her full skirt as she smiled automatically in response to a greeting from someone she knew.

"Merry, everything is going beautifully!" Mrs. Devore clutched Merry's arm in emphasis. She had raised her voice more than necessary to compete with the band that had just returned from a fifteen-minute break and was now in the middle of a swinging rock-and-roll number made famous by Elvis Presley. "Thank God I decided to let you do everything. I'd be a nervous wreck if I'd had to handle any more than I did."

Merry smiled at the gray-haired woman who looked so uncomfortable in a man's shirt and tight jeans cuffed to show bobby socks and black-and-white saddle oxfords that had obviously been purchased specifically for this occasion—probably from a store that specialized in cheerleader accessories, Merry thought with a silent chuckle. This was the first time Merry had seen the bank vice president dressed in anything other than expensive business suits. "I'm glad you're pleased, Mrs. Devore."

"Of course I'm pleased. You do all the work and I'll get the credit," the woman replied with a sly smile. "But just to show my gratitude, I must remind you that I want you to feel like a guest tonight. Enjoy yourself, find a dance partner, mingle with the other club members. You know how we'd love to have you join our club."

"I'll try to come to the next meeting," Merry promised.

"You do that. Now have that dance, Merry, and relax for a few minutes. Everything is going just fine." Mrs. Devore smiled at her and then rushed away to speak to other guests.

Smiling at the older woman's warm enthusiasm, Merry turned only to find herself practically in Grant's arms. "Didn't I hear your client order you to dance?" he inquired with interest.

Merry frowned at him. "She didn't say it had to be with you."

Grant only laughed and took her arm. "May I have the pleasure, Miss James?"

She admitted to herself, if not to Grant, that she would dearly love to dance with him. "Yes, Mr. Bryant, you may," she said resignedly.

Grinning broadly, Grant led her onto the dance floor. Merry made no attempt to hide her moan when the band immediately began to play "Love me Tender," the lead singer crooning in a sultry Presley imitation that sent chills down Merry's back. Why couldn't they have followed "Hound Dog" with "Blue Suede Shoes"? she asked herself as Grant took her into his arms. Was everyone conspiring against her?

"So how much did you have to pay Mrs. Devore to order me to dance?" Merry asked Grant with exaggerated suspicion, hoping to divert her own thoughts from the way his solid body felt pressed so closely against hers.

If possible, he held her even closer, a low chuckle rumbling in his chest, which vibrated against her. "I had nothing to do with that. I swear."

"But you didn't waste any time turning it to your advantage, did you?" Merry grumbled.

"I don't believe in wasting time, boss," Grant returned smoothly, his left hand sliding just fractionally toward the curve of her derriere. "That's what makes me such a good—" he paused to grin tauntingly before completing the sentence "—employee."

As he had obviously intended, Merry was quite sure that Grant was good in more ways than one. She glared at him when his hand dipped lower, though she knew his action was hidden by the near darkness of the shadowy corner he'd led her to. Whose clever idea had it been to lower the lights so dramatically whenever the band played an old love song? She glumly suspected that it had been hers. Anything to set the mood, she'd said. What she was rapidly getting in the mood for hadn't been in her plans at the time.

"You feel so good in my arms. Small and feminine and soft. I could hold you like this all night."

Merry swallowed a moan as a quiver went through her at his husky words. "I'm too short for slow dancing," she managed to say, trying to ease the sexual tension building between them with light conversation. "Even though you're not quite six feet, I just come to your shoulder, especially in these saddle oxfords. Wouldn't you rather be dancing with someone cheek-to-cheek?"

"There's no one in the world I'd rather be dancing with," he assured her, resting his cheek against her head. "You're perfect for me."

"I'll, uh . . ." *Come on, Merry, say something sensible! Don't let him do this to you!* "I'll bet you say that to all the girls."

Well, hell. Was that the most original thing she could come up with? she asked herself in despair. She usually had no trouble thinking of something to say to defuse an awkward situation. How did Grant turn her into such an idiot?

He laughed softly and guided her into the very darkest part of the corner where they were dancing. "There *are* no other girls, Merry, love. Only you."

"Don't give me that line. Grant, get your hand off my—"

"The band is very good," he interrupted smoothly. "Are they local?"

"Yes," she answered grudgingly.

"I've always liked this song." His words were a seductive murmur, audible only to her. His cheek rubbed slowly against her hair. "It's schmaltzy, but still kind of sexy. Have you ever made out to this song?"

Merry's eyes drifted closed. Her senses were filled almost to overflowing by the feel of him, the warmth of him, the crisp, citrusy smell of him. "I, uh, don't think so."

His mouth nuzzled against her temple. "Would you like to?"

She swallowed a moan, then a hysterical chuckle as she realized that Grant was trying to seduce her on a crowded dance floor, right in front of the cream of Springfield society. And, oh, God, he was succeeding! Her palms were damp, her breathing shaky, her pulse racing. She wanted nothing more than to drag him into a broom closet and throw herself all over him. *Oh, Merry*, she moaned silently. *Where is your willpower?*

"Don't do this, Grant," she whispered, her voice strained.

That errant hand tightened against the upper curve of her bottom, pressing her more fully into his abdomen. If Merry's physical reactions to his seduction were evident to him, his were equally apparent to her. Instinct had told her he wanted her from the moment their eyes had first met in her office the day before. Now his body confirmed that knowledge, seconded by his husky voice. "I want you, Merry," he murmured for her ears alone. "You know that, don't you?"

"Yes."

Her candid admission seemed to please him, and to encourage him. "It's not all one-sided, is it, honey? Am I imagining that you're attracted to me, as well?"

"You know I am," she moaned, burrowing her face into his shoulder. "But—"

"No 'buts,'" Grant broke in firmly. "You've told me all I needed to know. Now tell me that you'll finally have that dinner with me on your first free night."

She lifted her head and drew a deep breath, sudden panic stiffening her spine. He was only asking for a date, she reminded herself shakily. A simple date. Not so unexpected, considering what had just passed between them, what had been between them from the beginning. And yet she still panicked. "I, uh, I'll let you know."

Grant bit off a frustrated curse when the music suddenly stopped and the light brightened. Merry backed away from him, blinking as if she'd just awakened from a confusing dream. Grant glared at her. "We've got to talk," he informed her bluntly. "Let's go outside."

"No, I—"

"Please," he added, taking her arm. He kept his face impassive as she eyed him warily. Confused and increasingly annoyed by the mixed signals she gave him—admitting her attraction to him one moment and refusing to even have dinner with him the next—he fought the urge to just throw her over his shoulder and haul her outside for a confrontation. Finally she nodded and, without another word, he led her toward an exit.

A flagstone patio furnished with small, round, umbrella-shaded tables overlooked the golf course behind the country club. Grant did not spare a glance for the deserted, moonlight-silvered greens but turned his full attention to the petite woman in front of him as he backed her against a stone wall and loomed over her. "Okay, talk," he ordered.

"About what?" she demanded, impatience laced with uncertainty.

"About why you're running from me."

"I'm not—"

"Merry. Don't say you're not. You are. We met yesterday, we were attracted to each other, I asked you out, you turned me down."

"I told you, I—"

"Yes, you explained your reasons, but what's your excuse now? We've spent the day together, we've had a great time, you've admitted you're attracted to me, and yet you're still putting me off. I know you go out with other guys because I asked Melinda. She also told me that you're not involved with anyone else in particular, and haven't been in a long time."

"You asked my little sister about my love life?"

"You needn't look so outraged. I was desperate. I was trying to find out what I'm up against, but I still don't know. Why won't you give us a chance to see what there is between us other than physical attraction?"

"Grant, this is ridiculous."

"Why, Merry?"

She sighed in frustration. He wasn't going to give up without an explanation. And though his persistence annoyed her, she couldn't really say that she blamed him. He was right. The attraction between them *was* powerful, and obvious to both of them. Of course he couldn't understand why she was putting him off. She wasn't sure she understood herself. Except that . . . "You make me nervous," she found herself saying.

The soft patio lights cast a golden glow over Grant's look of surprise. "I make you nervous?" he repeated disbelievingly.

"Yes, you do," she reiterated shortly, her hands twisting in front of her. "You move too fast."

"I've always been the type to decide what I want fairly quickly and start working immediately to attain my goals," he admitted with a faint smile. "I've wanted you from the moment I first saw you. Being with you today has only reinforced my initial attraction to you. Holding back just to allow a more conventional time period to pass would be pointless."

"I guess you and I are different in that way. I'm more cautious. I have to take time to examine the consequences of my actions."

He stood silently for a moment, then lifted a hand to touch her cheek. "Who hurt you, Merry?"

It was extremely uncomfortable to be so open with a man, Merry decided. She didn't at all like this feeling that Grant could read her mind. "Oh, Grant, let's not go into the past now. I have a party to supervise."

"A party you can get back to in just a minute," he promised her, his fingers stroking the curve of her neck. "Please talk to me, Merry. Let me know what kind of dragon I have to face to win the princess."

Despite her resolution to resist him, she caught herself tilting her head so that her cheek rubbed his palm. She was hopeless where Grant Bryant was concerned. No willpower at all. "I'm no princess, Grant," she murmured at last. "Just a woman with a lot of responsibility. I'm the legal guardian of two teenagers and I run a business that takes a lot of my time right now. It's hard for some men to make allowances for those things."

"You're obviously speaking from experience."

"Yes. I was engaged when my parents were killed. Justin couldn't deal with suddenly becoming responsible for my younger brother and sisters. Matt was twenty, a junior in college, Marsha was a seventeen-year-old high-school senior and the twins were only nine. We were okay financially, thanks to my father's obsession with life insurance, for which I've been grateful, but the emotional costs were staggering. My brother and sisters were devastated, as I was. Justin found himself suddenly fifth on my list of priorities, and he couldn't take it. He eased out of our engagement only two months after the accident."

"And the men you've dated since?"

She shrugged slightly, looking out over the golf course. "They've been friends, nothing more. I didn't worry about going out with them because I knew that we would never become serious enough for my duties to become a problem. I'm *not* a martyr to my family," she added, her eyes meeting his as she realized how she sounded. "I have fun and I take time for myself when I need to. But I don't take on unnecessary complications."

"And I make you nervous because you see me as an unnecessary complication?" Grant asked gently.

"Maybe," she admitted.

"Because you know there's something between us other than friendship," he elaborated, moving closer to her. "Something powerful and irresistible. Something that could change both of our lives—has already changed them, in fact."

"No," she denied hastily, that odd sense of panic attacking her again as it had on the dance floor.

"No?" The word was only a whisper, a breath of sound that caressed her parted lips as he lowered his mouth to within an inch of hers.

"Yes," she murmured, no longer certain what the question had been. She'd been wanting him to kiss her again all day, she admitted to herself. She wanted him to kiss her now.

4

PERHAPS HE REALLY COULD read her mind. Grant closed the infinitesimal distance between their lips. The kiss was hungry, all-consuming. The kiss of lovers long separated, soulmates in discovery, two halves made whole. His lips shouldn't have felt so familiar, not after only one previous kiss. She felt as if she'd known him for a lifetime. Maybe longer.

The world was spinning. Merry twined her arms around Grant's neck, locking herself into the security of his embrace. The kiss went on for a very long time, and when they drew back for air, it was only for the briefest of moments. And then they were kissing again, greedy, insatiable. Merry heard a moan, unaware that it had come from her own throat until Grant's rumble of pleasure echoed the sound.

Lips clinging, tongues dancing, bodies quivering, they savored the sensations, soft breasts flattened against hard chest, feminine softness pressed to rigid masculinity. This need had been building from the moment they'd laid eyes on each other the day before.

The day before. Merry moaned again as she realized that she was plastered all over a man she'd known less than thirty hours, that she'd told him the story of her life and was now demonstrating quite graphically how much she wanted him. And hadn't she just been the one to tell him that she believed in proceeding cautiously?

Grant tore his mouth from hers, lifting her so that he could bury his face against the curve of her neck. "Merry," he muttered, his voice ragged, his breathing harsh and hot against her skin. "Oh, God, Merry."

She could feel him trembling. She closed her eyes tightly, feeling desired as she had never been before. There was something incredibly seductive in being wanted so badly. Once again Grant was making her feel special, alluring, infinitely desirable. No one had ever made her feel quite like this before. She tried to speak, but there were no words to express her feelings—the hunger, the need, the fear.

"Merry? Hey, Merry! Sorry to break this up, but we need you inside for a minute."

Merry gasped and pushed herself out of Grant's arms as a young male voice penetrated her foggy consciousness. Lifting cold, shaking hands to her hot, flushed cheeks, she turned to Kirk, the broadly grinning young employee she'd known since he'd been in diapers because his family lived just down the street from her house. "What is it, Kirk?"

"Inside," Kirk repeated slowly, teasingly pointing a finger toward the door. "Nothing major, but we need the boss. Think you can tear yourself away?"

"I, uh . . ." Oh, God, where was her strength, her dignity? She straightened her shoulders and dropped her hands to her side. "Where?" she asked curtly.

"Kitchen," Kirk replied. "Come on, I'll show you the way."

Avoiding Grant's eyes, Merry moved toward the door. "I know the way."

"Yeah, but I think you're a little disoriented," Kirk returned, tossing his shaggy sandy hair out of his eyes and throwing a thumbs-up sign at Grant behind Merry's back. "Can't imagine why, can you?"

"Kirk," Merry said warningly, reaching for the door and telling herself it didn't matter that she'd just been caught by one of her young employees in totally unprofessional behavior. She was lying, of course. It did matter to her.

"Merry."

She paused, wetting her slightly swollen lips as she looked back at Grant. "Yes?"

"I can handle it."

She knew what he meant. He was telling her he wasn't Justin, that he could deal with her responsibilities. She only wished she could believe him. "I have to go, Grant," she told him in little more than a whisper, then hurried inside.

Grant lingered for a while outside, taking deep breaths of the crisp, evening springtime air as he waited until he could return inside without embarrassing himself. His jeans had been tight when he'd put them on; they were painfully so now. He'd been staggered by the depths of passion hidden behind that wall of cool professionalism she had erected around herself. Staggered and overjoyed. Somehow he had known the passion was there, had known from the beginning. Just as he'd known that he was the one who could bring it out.

So now he knew what he was fighting.

Grant had become a workaholic to prove something to himself, and to a father who had demanded too much from a son born to parents over forty, a son he'd never expected to have, born eleven years after Leida.

Merry, on the other hand, hid behind her work to protect herself from being hurt again. Her fiancé's defection must have been more painful than she was willing to admit. The bastard. What kind of idiot could walk away from Merry's love, leave her when she needed him most? And now Grant had to fight the other man's stupidity, to convince Merry that he wasn't a weak coward, afraid of complicating his life, or a selfish jerk, refusing to share her with the family she loved so deeply.

It was going to take determination, which Grant had in abundance, and patience, of which he had never had enough. He wanted her more than he'd ever wanted any woman. There was no doubt in his dazed mind that she was the only woman he'd ever want in the future. He wasn't quite noble enough to settle for fifth or sixth place with her, but he wouldn't mind so badly sharing first place with her family. He liked her family, having met all of them except Marsha. No problems there. All he had to do was convince Merry.

"Yeah, that's all," he muttered, easing his fingertips into the front pocket of his jeans, relieved to feel the fabric loosening a bit. "No problem, right?"

"Like hell."

FRIDAY WAS the most hectic day in the history of MerryMakers. Wouldn't you know, Merry thought as she pushed a hand through her disheveled hair late that afternoon, that she'd have her busiest day when she was least equipped to handle it. Things had been going wrong all day. Shipments delayed, orders confused, decorating rushed. To add to the confusion, the caterer had thought the banquet that evening began at eight, when it actually began at seven. Thank God she had thought to confirm everything late this afternoon, Merry reflected wearily.

Because he worried about Merry while Marsha was still recuperating, Matt had stopped by to check on things during the afternoon, only to end up in another heated argument with Melinda and Meaghan. Merry had been prepared to step in and take care of it when Grant had somehow resolved the situation before anyone had realized he had interceded. Though she knew she should be grateful for Grant's help, Merry found herself resenting his interference. For so long she had been the one to whom her family turned; it was hard to accept the fact that she wasn't needed to handle everything.

To top off her day, Grant was slowly but surely driving her crazy. Not that he'd done anything overtly to disturb her. He had shown up at nine o'clock and gone quietly to work helping Merry and Kirk put away the props they'd used the night before. He never once mentioned the scene outside the country club, for which she tried to be grateful. But she couldn't help wondering whether their kisses had been as devastating to him as they had been to her. She'd managed to avoid him for the rest of the evening, and he'd made no further effort to confront her. Now, after a near-sleepless night, she felt like a wrung-out washcloth, but Grant looked as if he'd gotten a long, restful night's sleep.

All day he'd been treating her with much the same slightly amused indulgence he displayed toward the twins, and Merry was getting damned tired of it. Even as she told herself that she was pleased he'd backed off, some perversely feminine part of her wanted him to at least appear to have some difficulty in staying an arm's length away from her. Was she the only one who was having to fight to keep her hands to herself?

Only once had she caught him looking at her with what she could almost interpret to be raw hunger—and that had been when he'd glanced up from the typewriter to find her staring at him in what she strongly suspected had been exactly the same way.

She was sitting at her desk, scowling at a stack of invoices, when Melinda spoke from the doorway. "Meaghan and I are going now unless you need us for anything else. Kirk's giving us a ride home."

Merry shook her head. "No, go on. I'll be home after the banquet, probably around ten. Remember, I said it was okay for Savage to come over and watch a movie with you tonight, but show some consideration for Marsha, will you? Keep the noise down."

"Believe me, we won't be doing much laughing. Not with Meaghan's date, Boring Boyd, there with us."

"Melinda, you really shouldn't talk about your sister's new boyfriend that way."

"Why not? She makes fun of Savage. Besides, Boyd *is* boring."

Actually, there wasn't a whole lot more that Merry could say. Meaghan *did* make fun of Savage, and even Merry thought Boyd was boring. She'd never figured out what Meaghan saw in the arrogant young man. Oh, well, she mused, she'd done her duty by trying to reprove Melinda. She turned her mind back to business. "Have Linda and Louis called in yet?"

"Yeah, they both said they'd be on time to help out."

"Good. That's everyone I need tonight." She opened her desk drawer and pulled out some money. "Here, take this and ask Kirk if he'll stop for chicken on the way home. Be sure to get enough to feed everyone. Marsha is feeling much better, but I told her not to worry about dinner."

"Chicken sounds good to me," Melinda replied carelessly, slipping the folded bill into a pocket of her bright yellow jeans. "Oops, there goes the phone again."

"It's okay. I've got it," Grant said from behind her. He'd been on his way into Merry's office, but he turned back to pick up the receiver, waving goodbye to Kirk and the twins as they hurried out, eager to escape. Merry's sisters helped with the business because they chose to—and because Merry paid them minimum wage, which provided them with money for records, makeup and fast food—but they were normal kids, with normal interests outside of business and school. They welcomed the weekend with noisy enthusiasm.

A moment later Grant stood in the door to Merry's office, unsmiling. "It's someone named Joe Borden," he informed her. "He wants to talk to you. He said it was a personal call."

"Thank you, Grant," Merry replied, perversely pleased that he looked jealous. She lifted the receiver. "Hi, Joe. How's it going?"

Merry had grown up with Joe, and they'd dated occasionally during the past year since his divorce. Their relationship was more one of convenience than anything else; they were comfortable with each other and had a pleasant time together when one or the other needed a date for a special occasion. Lately Joe had shown a few signs of wanting the relationship to go further, but Merry had not encouraged him. She liked Joe, but her feelings for him were not in the least romantic. Not at all like those she felt for . . .

She pulled her thoughts sternly away from the man still standing in the doorway and tried to concentrate on the man who was even now asking her out for dinner the next night. "I'm sorry, Joe, I can't tomorrow night. We're booked for a retirement party. The man went to work for his company in 1946 so they want a forties' theme, which means we'll have a couple of hours of decorating, and then another couple to take it all down afterward. Yes, I know I've been busy lately, Joe, but it couldn't be helped. Yes, Marsha's feeling much better. I'm looking forward to having her back. I could use a couple of nights off," she added with a laugh.

Grant was still glowering at her. She glared back as she listened to Joe. "Sunday night?" As it happened, she was free Sunday night. Her eyes locked with Grant's. He wasn't actually ordering her to turn down the date, she decided, but he certainly was sending negative messages with those icy blue eyes. She really should accept the date with Joe. She probably would have had she never met Grant. But she *had* met Grant, and—as he had insisted the night before—everything had changed. "I'm sorry, Joe, I can't. But thank you for asking."

Grant smiled at her, an approving, sexy smile that hit her like a blow to the stomach. She was hardly conscious of saying goodbye to Joe before she replaced the receiver. She immediately went on the defensive, trying to counteract the effects of that smile. "Hasn't anyone ever told you that it's not polite to listen in on private telephone conversations?"

Still leaning against the doorframe, he continued to smile, ignoring her words. "You didn't really want to go out with him, did you, Merry?"

She snatched up a box of pink tapers from one corner of her desk and brushed past him on her way to the largest stockroom, deciding that Grant wasn't the only one who could ignore a question he didn't want to answer. "It's after five, Grant," she told him over her shoulder. "I'm sure Leida is expecting you."

"Leida never gets home before six," Grant replied imperturbably, following her into the large, prop-crowded room. His gaze moved automatically toward the huge,

Arabian Nights pillows before he turned sternly away.
No sense indulging in fantasies just now. They could wait
until later in the evening, when he was alone and missing her. "Are you going home before the banquet?"

"No. I have a few more things to do, then I'll change
here and go on over to the hotel."

"The banquet doesn't start until seven, does it?"

"No. I'll need to be there by six-thirty, though." She
rose onto her toes to slide the box of candles onto a high
shelf. Grant's hand was there immediately to help, making her vividly aware that he stood mere inches behind
her, touching her only with his warmth. She closed her
eyes. That was all it took, she mused pensively. All day
she'd tried to resist him, and yet all he had to do was stand
close to her and she could think of nothing but touching
him, being held by him, kissing him.

His hand fell from the shelf to her shoulder, curving
there to hold her gently. "Do you know how long this day
has been for me?" he murmured, both his hands now
resting on her shoulders. "How hard it has been for me
to be near you without touching you?"

"Oh, Grant," she sighed, and there was surrender in
her voice. He heard it. Turning her in his arms, he lowered his mouth to hers. It was almost as if the hours between last night and this moment had never taken place.
Merry thought her body had cooled from the fever Grant
had aroused in her last night, but even now she felt herself going into flames in his arms. And the kiss had barely
begun.

As if he had all the time in the world, Grant kissed her
lingeringly, skillfully exploring every centimeter of her
mouth. Merry arched into him, loving what he was
doing but needing so much more. Pressed almost painfully into his chest, her breasts strained against the lace

of her bra, aching for his touch. For the first time she was glad that he seemed able to read her so easily when his hand slipped between them to cup her through the nubby cotton knit of her red sweater. His long fingers kneaded gently, easing her ache in some ways, yet making her even more anxious to feel his hands on her bare skin.

Wanting him to know the same needs she felt, she loosened a middle button of his white oxford shirt and slipped her fingertips inside to stroke his chest, toying with the crisp curls she discovered there. Grant moaned softly against her mouth and lowered his hand to the hem of her sweater, pushing underneath so that his palm was flat against her taut stomach. Dropping her head back, her eyes closed, Merry inhaled sharply when his hands moved upward to touch her through the thin lace bra. Even then he held back, rubbing and stroking through the fabric until her nipples were hard points of need and she was burning with hunger for more.

She had his shirt almost completely open now. Her hand circled restlessly over him, sliding down his ribs, stroking his flat stomach, then moving upward to toy with the hard nubs she discovered beneath the soft hair. Seeming to grow tired of touching her through fabric, Grant searched out the front clasp of her bra and released it.

Merry almost cried out when he took one distended nipple between his fingers and rolled it gently, tugging lightly to heighten the sensation. She'd thought his touch would soothe her pain, but now she ached all over. "Grant, what are you doing to me?" she moaned, her hands clenching inside his shirt.

"I hope I'm making you want me just a fraction as much as I want you," he replied, his voice ragged.

She opened clouded eyes and looked up at him, noting the sheen of perspiration on his upper lip, the dark flush on his high cheekbones, the hot flames in his iceblue eyes. "How much do you want me, Grant?" she heard herself asking him.

In answer he pulled her closer, one hand pressing into the small of her back so that she was held hard against his arousal. "More than I've ever wanted anyone . . . or anything," he muttered, dropping his cheek to the top of her head.

"Then you already know how much I want you," she whispered into his shoulder.

"Oh, God." He cupped the back of her head in one large hand, threading his fingers into her dark shoulder-length hair, tilting her face back for his kiss. He kissed her thoroughly, yet with such tenderness that her eyes filled with tears. Slanting his mouth to a new angle, he kissed her again, this time with a hunger that bordered on desperation. He drew back fractionally, his breathing labored, to murmur, "We'd better stop this while I still can."

Clinging to him, Merry decided that she might as well try to stop breathing as to step out of his arms now. She reached for his tie, which hung crookedly over his unbuttoned shirt, and began to loosen it.

"Merry, honey, I want you so badly I hurt," Grant warned her. "Don't expect me to be too noble."

"So who asked you to be noble?"

"Uh . . ." His head was beginning to spin. He cleared his throat. "We *are* in your office, you know."

"Mmm-hmm. The front door's locked."

"The, uh," He broke off when she pressed her mouth to the racing pulse in the hollow of his throat. "The cleaning crew?" he asked, his voice raw.

She gave him one of her slightly lopsided smiles and dangled his tie from her fingers. "The cleaning crew comes in on Tuesdays, Thursdays and Saturdays. This is Friday." Her smile faded as her gaze met his, the slight shyness and vulnerability she'd tried to conceal clearly evident in their depths. "Didn't you just tell me last night that you don't believe in wasting time?" she asked in a husky murmur.

One corner of his mouth deepened into a half smile. "I think I may have said something to that effect. But you said you wanted to proceed with caution. I don't want to rush you."

Merry pulled his shirt out of the waistband of his slacks, sliding her hands up to his shoulders beneath the crisp fabric. "You're not rushing me," she told him in little more than a whisper. "I'm rushing myself. I want you so much that for the first time in years I can't seem to be cautious."

Grant fell in love with her at that moment. Or maybe he'd been in love with her from the moment he'd seen her, he mused, reaching up to cup her face between his hands. So much depth, so much passion in such a tiny package, he thought wonderingly, his thumbs caressing her delicate cheekbones.

Her hands resting on his shoulders, Merry stood very still, watching the play of emotions on Grant's handsome face. He was looking at her as if she were the most beautiful woman he'd ever seen, with such delight, such reverence. Again she was forced to blink back tears. How could she resist this man, who looked at her this way?

She could not.

There were no considerations of past or present complications, no questioning the short length of time they'd known each other. Only needs and desire and caring.

Merry moistened her lips, consciously inviting him back to them. Grant accepted the invitation gratefully.

This kiss was different. They both knew, this time, that they would not be stopping with a kiss. Grant took his time, stretching the embrace into a leisurely exploration that reassured her even as it fed the growing excitement in her. All trace of hesitation, of tentativeness was gone. Instead, he kissed her as if he had every right, as if she belonged to him, and he to her. At that point Merry would not have argued with either assumption.

She stepped out of her shoes, lowering her height by well over an inch. Grant chuckled as she tilted her head back to look at him. "You're so little," he told her softly.

"I've always wanted to be tall and voluptuous," she confessed ruefully. "I'm still waiting to grow up."

"Haven't you realized yet that I think you're perfect?" He kissed her again, his hands going to the hem of her sweater. "Perfect," he repeated as he swept the red knit garment over her head and removed her unclasped bra.

Flushing a little, Merry bit her lower lip, wondering if her lack of size would displease him when he noted that it applied to her breasts, as well. But far from looking dissatisfied, Grant caught his breath and raised his hands to touch her. He circled her already-hard nipples with his fingers, then dropped to his knees to taste them.

Her hands cupping his head, Merry arched unconsciously, her head falling back so that her hair cascaded over her bare shoulders. Her knees went weak as Grant laved her breasts with his tongue, then threatened to buckle when he gently nipped at her. His hands clenched her hips, holding her upright while he trailed kisses down her stomach to the waistband of her floral skirt. The skirt fell in a colorful pool around her ankles, followed rapidly by her sheer panty hose. Merry stood before him

clad only in tiny red panties, feeling like a pagan priest-
ess as he continued to kneel before her as if in awe.

She tugged at his shoulders. "Kiss me again, Grant.
Please."

He rose quickly, sweeping her into his arms for another deep, richly satisfying kiss, offering his tongue in
a tantalizing preview of an intimacy yet to come. Returning the kiss with everything she had, Merry tugged
impatiently at his clothing, wanting nothing between
them.

He stood unselfconscious before her when she'd divested him of every last scrap of fabric, allowing her to
admire him for as long as she wished. She looked her fill,
finding no fault with his body. He was beautiful, she
thought wonderingly. Broad shoulders, powerful chest,
tight waist, narrow hips. He was a strong man, proudly
and heavily aroused. She held out her arms to him.

THE HUGE SATIN PILLOWS were almost unbearably sensuous against skin already sensitized by Grant's thorough exploration. Just as she'd examined him with her
eyes, and then with her hands, so he explored her now,
finding all her secrets and painstakingly memorizing
them. Merry's hair lay in a dark fan against the lush
purple fabric as she arched into Grant's skillful caresses.

"You're so beautiful. So perfect," Grant murmured
against the soft, moist skin of her abdomen. His lips
rubbed adoringly across her. "Are you protected,
Merry?"

"Yes, Grant," she whispered brokenly, driven nearly
mad by his agonizingly slow caresses, "please love me
now. I can't wait any longer."

He pulled himself upward until his lips were against
hers. "Are you very sure, Merry?"

How could he even ask now, when she'd been demonstrating so boldly how very sure she was? "Yes. Yes, *please*, Grant. Now."

His fingers finding the proof of her readiness he gave in to her sensual demands. Merry cried out softly as he entered her, slowly, tenderly. But it was not tenderness she wanted from him. Not now. Her hands gripped him, recklessly urging him on, pushing him past the point of control until he was moving as frantically as she, driving them ruthlessly toward the violent explosion they both wanted, needed.

Merry clung fiercely to him, feeling almost as if they had left the ground somehow and she would fall if she didn't hold on. Her fingernails left tiny crescents in Grant's arching shoulders, but the resulting stinging seemed only to encourage him. Higher and higher he took her, until together they reached the steepest possible point of pleasure. Hovering there as long as they could, they gasped in unison, the mingled sound one of joy and release. And then they slowly, slowly drifted downward, still joined, still clinging as if they would never let go.

She'd thought she knew what it was like, Merry mused much later, her cheek snuggled into the hollow of Grant's shoulder. She'd thought the pleasant, relaxed state she'd known in the past had been the peak of sexual pleasure. How wrong she had been. Making love with Grant had been a revelation, a discovery of feelings and sensations she could never have imagined. He'd been so generous, so considerate. He'd made sure that she was protected— she was suddenly grateful that her doctor had recently prescribed birth-control pills to regulate her menstrual cycle—then had ensured her pleasure before finding his own. Somehow she'd known he would be a wonderful lover. She hadn't been disappointed.

Staring up at the red-and-blue tissue-paper liberty bell suspended over their heads, Grant pulled Merry closer. It was new, he thought, almost in awe. All new. He had never felt this way before. He hadn't planned to make love with her this soon. All he'd wanted was to talk her into going out with him, to get to know him. But he wasn't sorry. How could he be? He only hoped that Merry wasn't regretting their impulsive lovemaking. He was almost afraid to speak, afraid to find out. What if she withdrew from him now, after what they'd just shared?

Grant was being so quiet. Merry wondered what he was thinking. She lifted her head from his shoulder to look at him. "Well?"

Smiling, he brushed back a lock of hair that clung to her perspiration-moistened cheek. "Well, what?"

"Why aren't you saying anything? You've never been at a loss for words with me."

He chuckled. "Would you believe I'm scared?"

"No," she replied promptly, propping herself up on one elbow, her head cradled in her hand.

"Well, I am."

"Scared of what?"

"Of finding out that you're sorry about what just happened between us. Of discovering that you hate me for rushing you into something you weren't ready for."

She touched his cheek with her free hand, softening at the vulnerability she found in his eyes. "You didn't exactly force me, Grant. I practically ripped the clothes from your body, or had you forgotten?"

He grinned. "No, I remember that quite clearly."

She sobered, searching for adequate words. "I'm not sorry we made love, Grant. It was beautiful . . . and, I think, inevitable. But . . ."

"But?" he prompted in a murmur.

Merry sighed. "I don't know what you expect from me now," she admitted. "When it comes right down to it, we're still practically strangers.

"You and I were never strangers, Merry," he informed her emphatically. "But you needn't worry. I know what you're trying to say. You don't want to be rushed more than you already have been. I understand."

"You do?"

"Yes. I'll give you time to adjust to us. To being part of an 'us,'" he elaborated with a smile. "I'm not going to insist that you make any sudden and dramatic changes in your life, other than allowing me a place there."

"And you don't call that sudden and dramatic?" she asked in quick amusement. "My life changed dramatically the day you walked into my office, Grant Bryant. Just look at me."

His raised one eyebrow. "I *am* looking at you, honey. You're gorgeous."

She flushed a little at his all-encompassing smile. "That's not what I mean, and you know it. But seriously, Grant, I want you to understand that my life is really very hectic just now. Spring is the busiest season—other than Christmas—for the business and for the twins at school. I can't afford to neglect my business or my family."

"I'm not asking you to neglect either of them," Grant answered gently. "All I'm asking is that you make time for me. Not a lot of time—just a little, if that's all you have to give for now. That's enough for a beginning."

"A beginning?"

He pulled her on top of him and pressed his lips to hers before speaking against them. "The beginning of a long, wonderful relationship."

Merry's tiny spurt of unease vanished in the delight of his kiss. She was tempted to allow the embrace to continue for a long time, as it showed signs of doing, but she reluctantly acknowledged the call of duty. "I have to get ready for the banquet now, Grant. I'm going to be late if I don't hurry."

He had just told her that he wouldn't hold her back from her responsibilities, Grant reflected ruefully. Too bad he hadn't mentioned that to certain parts of his body that were even now urging him to delay her just a little longer. "All right," he told her, exaggerating a grudging sigh to make her smile. He was pleased when she did. "Sure you don't need me to help out tonight?"

"I'm sure, but thanks for offering." She kissed him swiftly, then pushed herself out of his arms, somewhat self-consciously gathering her clothes before hurrying into the adjoining dressing room.

Grateful for her insistence a year earlier that they have a small shower stall put in for the convenience of anyone who wanted to change into costume at the office, she showered quickly and dressed in the cream-colored business suit with fuchsia silk blouse that she'd brought with her that morning. She applied makeup swiftly and expertly, highlighting her slightly slanted green eyes and fine cheekbones. As she outlined her lips with a pencil, she fought a smile. It had suddenly occurred to her that she was calmly preparing for an evening's work after taking a step that her instincts told her would change her life forever. She should be filled with doubts, anxieties, maybe even regrets, but she had never felt better in her life. Grant's cheerful acceptance of life's odd twists and turns seemed to be rubbing off on her, she decided, rather liking the sexy, bold, almost wicked feelings that lingered from their lovemaking. She was suddenly filled with optimism that they may, after all, have a chance for a "long, wonderful relationship."

5

"WHATCHA DOING, Uncle Grant?"

Grant looked up from the calculator and legal pad in front of him and smiled at his sixteen-year-old nephew. A handsome young man of athletic build with his father's brown-black hair and his mother's light blue eyes, Chip seemed to be enjoying his uncle's extended visit very much. Grant regretted for a moment that he hadn't had more time to spend with the boy since Leida's husband, Ian, had decided that family life wasn't for him and had taken off in search of adventure. That had been when Chip was six; Chip hadn't seen his father since. "Hi, Chip. I was just getting some figures together."

"Figures for what?" Chip came into the dining room Grant had commandeered as a temporary office and peered over his uncle's shoulder at the pad covered with neatly written numbers.

"Projected expenses and income from a computer consulting business," Grant answered patiently. He turned off the calculator and leaned back in the Hepplewhite dining chair. "What are you up to today?"

"Not much. Had ball practice earlier this morning, but now I'm free for the rest of the day. I thought maybe you'd want to do something with me."

Grant pushed himself away from the table and stood. "Okay. What should we do?"

The boy's face lit up. "Hey, you mean it? I'd understand if you're too busy. Really."

"I'm not too busy," Grant assured him. Never again, he thought firmly. Never again would he put business ahead of family. Their time together was too brief as it was. "What would you like to do today?" he asked again.

Chip's brow creased in thought, and Grant had to suppress a chuckle at the seriousness of his nephew's expression. As if it were a world-shaking decision, he thought indulgently. As it had all morning, his mind wandered for a moment to Merry. He wondered what she was doing now. She'd been at her office when he'd talked to her on the telephone earlier. He'd repeated the offer of his services, but she'd firmly declined. Something told him that she was deliberately putting some space between them after the unexpected turn their relationship had taken the day before. He couldn't really blame her, but he was amazed at how much he already missed her.

He was glad that Chip had suggested spending the day together. It would give Grant something to do besides stare at columns of numbers and think of Merry. He'd been having problems with his usually controllable libido since he'd first set eyes on Merry James. Replaying their fantastic lovemaking in his mind all day would be nothing short of sheer torture.

"Well?" he prompted with a grin when Chip still didn't speak up. "What'll it be, kid?"

"We could cruise in your Ferrari and pick up women," Chip suggested with an impish grin that most people would immediately recognize as very similar to his uncle's.

"Try again," Grant answered, managing not to laugh.

"Want to go float the Niangua?" Chip asked, naming a relatively slow-moving scenic river some twenty-five miles north of Springfield. "We can rent a canoe for the afternoon."

"You're on. Just give me a few minutes to change into jeans and sneakers."

"All right!" Chip leaped up and punched the air in his excitement. "I'll go tell Mom," he exclaimed, dashing from the room in a streak of red T-shirt and white Reeboks.

Pleased with Chip's enthusiasm for the impromptu outing, Grant gathered his papers and carried them with him to his room, deciding to give Tim a call later and offer another business partnership. He figured his friend would be tired of lying on beaches by now and ready to dive into a new project. In the meantime, a leisurely float trip would give Grant and Chip time to talk and get to know each other better. Somewhat guiltily realizing that Chip had craved a strong male influence in his life despite Leida's excellent care, Grant intended to play a prominent role in his nephew's life for the next few years.

Grinning, he thought of the similar role he intended to play in Merry's twin sisters' lives. Perhaps it was a bit early to be planning his wedding, he thought humorously, but that it would happen was inevitable in his mind. He was in love with Merry James, and he wanted her to have a permanent place in his life. Now all he had to do was convince her.

He pulled on a pair of jeans and reached for his white canvas deck shoes. "I'm hurrying, Chip!" he yelled in response to Chip's impatient summons, deliberately turning his thoughts back to the present.

ALTHOUGH SHE'D BEEN the one to ask him to stay away that day, the truth was Merry missed Grant terribly on Saturday. She thought of him frequently during the day—during the three hours she put in at the office before lunch and several times as she did her weekend shopping and other chores. She found it rather unnerving to acknowledge how much a part of her life he had become in such a short time. A week earlier she would not have imagined such a thing could happen—people did not meet and fall in love in a matter of days, she would have said. Yet these feelings she had for Grant were suspiciously akin to love, if not the real thing. Had she asked him to stay away because she'd truly been busy—or because she was still nervous about what was happening between them?

She woke thinking of him Sunday morning, which wasn't at all surprising since she'd dreamed of him all night. In fact, those dreams had been so vivid, so explicit, that she blushed scarlet when she walked into church that morning and found herself face-to-face with Grant. Since she'd been attending the same church with Leida for years, she'd wondered earlier if Grant would accompany his sister this morning. The thought had made her tremble in anticipation.

"Merry!" he exclaimed, obviously surprised to see her. "I didn't expect to see you here."

"I've been attending this church since I was in the nursery," she answered, her voice rather breathless. She smiled a greeting at Leida, standing at Grant's side, then remembered Marsha, who was waiting impatiently for an introduction. "Grant, this is my sister Marsha."

Marsha smiled brightly, her gray eyes scrutinizing the man who'd made such an impact on her family, and her elder sister, in particular. Now that she was almost entirely over her bout with the flu, Marsha was her old self—sharp, observant, quietly teasing. "I'm so glad to meet you, Grant."

Grant gave her one of his wonderful smiles, and Merry tried very hard not to be jealous that someone else was the recipient of that smile. *Oh, great, Merry,* she thought in disgust, *first you were jealous of Grant and Melinda, and now Grant and Marsha!*

"Grant!" A delighted twin entered the church lobby and rushed to the side of her new friend. "Hi!"

"Hello, gorgeous," he replied, giving her a quick hug that was as natural as if he'd known her for years.

"Uh-huh. You only called me that because you don't know which twin I am," the teenager accused him, though her pretty face was flushed with pleasure."

"Wrong. I called you that because you're gorgeous," he answered firmly, looking with approval at her conservatively fashionable lavender dress. Then, with smug self-confidence, he added, "Meaghan."

While everyone else laughed at Meaghan's openmouthed surprise, Grant's sister shook her head in amazement. "How in the world did you do that?" Leida demanded. "I've been going to church with this family for some time, and I still can't tell the twins apart!"

"Talent," Grant replied with a grin. He held back as the others entered the sanctuary, one hand unobtrusively holding Merry's arm. "I missed you yesterday," he said, his voice too quiet to be heard by the people going in around them. "Chip and I had a good time together, but I thought of you all day."

"I, uh..." Merry moistened her lips and looked up at him, deciding not to pursue that particular line. "How *did* you know it was Meaghan?" she asked instead.

He chuckled. "I can tell by their personalities. Melinda's delightfully brash, uninhibited, cocky. Meaghan's a bit quieter, a little more shy. They're both great kids, but they're quite different once you get to know them."

A bit startled at his accurate perception, Merry nodded. "Yes, they are." She looked beyond him at the flow of people going into the sanctuary. "We should go in now."

"All right. I see Leida and Marsha are sitting together. That means you and I can do the same thing."

Merry could not quite hide her grimace.

"Does that mean you don't want to sit by me?" Grant demanded.

She shook her head quickly. "Of course not. It's just that I've known the people in this little church all my life, and if they see me sitting by a man, they'll be positive that we're engaged or something."

"They'll be right," Grant replied, unperturbed. At her frown, he added, "About the 'or something.'"

"Just don't say I didn't warn you," she answered, stepping into the church to hide the flush that had darkened her cheeks.

The next hour was painfully pleasant. Merry liked sitting shoulder to shoulder with Grant on the padded pew, Marsha and Leida beside her, the twins and Chip on the pew behind. She liked the sound of her throaty alto blending with his clear tenor during the hymns. She liked the way his arm slipped behind her to rest on the back of the pew during the pastor's sermon, and when their hands touched as they passed the collection plate. Pleasant—but painful. To be so close to him with the memories of Friday afternoon still fresh in her mind was an exquisite form of torture.

It seemed so natural to be with him, to have him almost part of her family. Even the speculative looks she received from the sweet little matchmakers in the congregation did not bother her. Indulging herself in pleasant daydreams, she deliberately ignored the frisson of warning that tried to get her attention. A tiny voice whispered to her that any man who could bring her this much pleasure this easily could also bring her great pain if she were not very, very careful, but this she ignored, as well.

Merry invited Grant to join her family for lunch after church, extending the invitation to Leida and Chip. Chip, it turned out, had already accepted an invitation to spend the afternoon with a friend's family, and Leida also declined, claiming she had some paperwork to attend to. Grant promptly accepted Merry's invitation.

Lunch was a lively affair, with the twins competing for Grant's attention while Merry, Marsha and Matt—who usually joined the rest of the family for Sunday lunch, though he no longer lived in the big frame house Luke and Nancy James had left to their five children—watched with indulgent amusement as Grant tried to split his attention both ways. Merry was pleased, again, to note how easily Grant fitted in with her family, how comfortable he seemed to be, how genuinely fond of the younger members. He didn't seem at all daunted by the size of the family or intimidated by the obvious closeness that existed between brother and sisters, as others had been.

Matt dropped his bombshell during dessert. "I have an announcement to make. I've been promoted." He could not quite hide the pride in his handsome young face.

"Again?" Meaghan murmured with a sigh, obviously wondering whether the newest promotion would make her older brother even more autocratic.

"Yes, again," Matt returned quellingly. "I'm the new assistant manager of the Amber Rose Hotel in Nashville."

Merry's fork paused halfway to her mouth. She lowered it slowly. "Nashville, Tennessee?"

"That's right." Matt looked at her, his green eyes almost apologetic. "They want me to start next Monday, a week from tomorrow. I'll be moving this week."

Merry was stunned. Only half hearing the twins' teasing cheers that their bossy older brother would be moving away, she realized that, after so many years as a close unit, her family was growing up, changing. The brother and sisters had not been separated by more than the few miles to Matt's apartment since the death of their parents. Her pleasant, safe life was changing too rapidly. Her gaze met Grant's across the table, and she suddenly wondered if she were ready for the changes that waited for her.

"SO WHAT DOES ONE DO after dinner on a Sunday evening in Springfield, Missouri?" Grant asked with a lazy smile as he turned the key in the ignition of his Ferrari.

Merry settled into the low seat of the powerful sports car and smiled back at him, knowing exactly what she would like to do with him. But there was one barrier. "I think we'd have a bit of a problem with 'your place or mine.'" she commented.

He nodded, his smile growing a bit shaky as he read the desire she knew must be reflected in her eyes. He tried to answer lightly. "True. At your place we'd have to go back on display for the amusement of your kid sisters, and at mine we'd have to do the same thing for my older sister. So you want to go parking?"

Merry laughed, wondering if the sound seemed as forced to him as it did to her. She was so close to him in the snug vehicle. All she had to do was shift her hand a bit to touch his thigh. She kept her hands firmly clasped in her lap as she answered his teasing question. "I haven't been parking in years. In fact, the popular make-out spot when I was in high school is now a shopping center. Used to be a romantic, secluded hideaway."

"I'm too old for making out in a car, anyway," Grant murmured. "I'm definitely going to start looking for a place of my own this week."

Merry moistened her lips as that statement sank in. She and Grant had spent the hours after lunch together, with her family for a while, and then alone over dinner at a popular local restaurant, but this was the first time he'd brought up any plans for the future. Their conversation so far had been amusing, light and carefully impersonal, despite the undertones of sexual tension that were always there between them. She realized only now that she had been the one to keep things that way. "Does that mean you're staying in Springfield?"

He slanted her a quizzically amused glance. "You thought maybe I was planning to leave?"

She shrugged and looked down at the white-knuckled fingers she was twisting in her lap. "I didn't know. I thought you were only here on vacation. You've lived in Colorado for a long time, haven't you?"

"Yeah. Grew up there. The only times I've been to Springfield in the past were to visit Leida after she married Ian and moved here almost twenty years ago. But she liked this area enough to stay on after she and Ian divorced, and I can see why. Seems like a nice place to live."

"You're being rather impulsive, aren't you? You didn't intend to settle here when you arrived last week, did you?"

"Not particularly. But I hadn't met you when I arrived last week." His tone was firm, matter-of-fact, as if there could be no question that he would leave Missouri now that he knew Merry was there.

"Grant . . ." Her voice was husky before it died away for lack of words.

He exhaled gustily as he parked the Ferrari in the parking lot of MerryMakers. Merry hadn't been surprised when he had turned into the drive of her office. After all, there was nowhere else for them to go if they wanted to be alone. And they did want to be alone.

Grant's hand brought her face around to him with a gentle but inexorable pressure. The one tall security light in the parking lot threw enough illumination into the dark, cozy interior of the vehicle for Merry to see the determination in Grant's narrowed eyes. "When are you going to admit that our meeting has changed both our lives, Merry James? How many times do I have to tell you that this is more than a vacation fling for me? What happened between us Friday was spontaneous, unplanned, but it was real and very, very special. Are you going to try to argue with that?"

She had to smile at the truculent sound of his question. "No, Grant, I'm not going to argue. I know our lovemaking was special. You don't really think I respond like that to anyone else, do you?"

He leaned over to kiss her lightly, a promise of more to come. Much more. "I know damned well you don't. You might as well stop running, love. You're already caught."

Caught. Merry swallowed hard. "Are we just going to sit here in your car," she asked in as normal a tone as possible under the circumstances, "or would you like to come in for a drink?"

"You've got something to drink in there?" Grant moved away from her and reached for his door handle.

"Soft drinks or coffee," she clarified wryly. "Nothing stronger, I'm afraid."

"Coffee sounds good." Grant swung himself out of the low car with a masculine grace that made her catch her breath. She was still admiring his fluid movements when he opened her door and reached in to help her out. He pulled her straight into his arms and kissed her thoroughly before draping his arm around her shoulders and urging her toward the building. "Got your keys?"

She could only nod, her voice seeming to have deserted her temporarily. At least, she hoped it was just temporary, she thought in bemusement as she handed Grant the key ring she'd extracted from an outside pocket of her leather handbag. His kisses always had the most unusual effect on her.

"Marsha coming back to work tomorrow?" Grant asked when the rich smell of dripping coffee filled the office.

Merry turned away from the coffee maker to look at him, trying to hide the unexpected twinge of nervousness she felt now that she was finally alone with him. He was lounging on the long, red imitation-leather sofa in the reception area under an abstract print in brilliant shades of purple and red. The bright colors contrasted dramatically with the pale blue dress shirt stretched intriguingly across Grant's broad chest and the dark blue suit slacks that were filled so nicely with his powerful thighs. He had long since shed his coat and tie, but still a suggestion of restrained, utterly masculine elegance lingered.

"Merry?" Grant repeated, interrupting her surreptitious survey. She flushed a bit at the knowing smile he wore—as if he knew exactly how attractive she found him. But then, how could he *not* know? she asked herself in resignation.

"Yes, Marsha's coming back tomorrow," she said finally, remembering his question. "As you noticed this afternoon, she's fully recovered from her flu and ready to come back to work."

"I like her. I like all of your family." Grant shifted on the sofa and draped one arm along its back. Merry's attention was drawn immediately to the invitingly empty place beside him, within the circle of that arm.

"They like you, too," she answered distractedly.

Grant patted the sofa beside him with his free hand. She needed no further urging. Moments later she was curled at his side, his arm around her, his other hand entwined with hers in his lap. "Matt shook you up with his announcement, didn't he?" Grant asked unexpectedly. "I could tell that you had a hard time accepting the fact that he's moving away."

"Yes. Since my parents died, the five of us have been so close. I guess I thought it would always be that way." Merry rested her cheek in the hollow of Grant's shoulder, her fingers tightening in his.

"Nashville's not so very far away," Grant told her encouragingly. "You'll stay close to your brother. After all, Leida and I have lived in different states for years, but we've always kept in touch."

"You're really moving to Missouri, Grant?" Merry asked suddenly, his words reminding her of their conversation in his car. "Permanently?"

"I have no reason to return to Colorado," he replied frankly. "The company's been sold, and I have no desire to take the new owners up on their offer of employment with them. I have an apartment there, but it's been little more than a place to sleep for the past few years. Tim's drifting around, trying to find out what life holds besides sixteen-hour workdays and computer printouts. I've been kicking around some ideas in my head for a new business that I think would go over well in this area. Leida and Chip, my only family, are here." He lowered his head to nuzzle her temple. "And you're here."

"Both . . ." She had to stop to clear her throat as tiny flames spread from the spot where he'd kissed her. "Both your parents are gone?"

"Yes. My mother died of breast cancer when I was in high school. Dad died three years ago. His heart gave out on a golf course."

"I'm sorry," she murmured, knowing exactly how it felt to lose both parents.

He kissed her lightly, the gesture telling her he acknowledged and appreciated her sympathy.

"There's no, um, no one special in Colorado?" Merry asked hesitantly, holding herself still beneath his caress with an effort. She wanted to ask him about the business he was considering, but somehow this question seemed more important at the moment.

"A woman, you mean?"

She kept her gaze down. "Yes."

"Merry." He waited until she looked at him before continuing. "Do you honestly think there's another woman in my life now?"

She released a breath she hadn't known she was holding and shook her head. "No. No, of course there's not. You wouldn't be with me now if there were."

"No, I wouldn't," he agreed, pleased by her admission.

"Was there ever anyone special?" she dared to ask, rationalizing the highly personal question by reminding herself that he knew all about Justin.

Grant hesitated, then shrugged. "There was someone for a while. A couple of years, actually. Her name was Dolores, and she was—is—attractive and bright and ambitious. She's an editor for a travel magazine published in Denver, and she gives as much—if not more—of herself to her career as I did to mine for so long. We had a lot in common, and our relationship was convenient for both of us. Neither of us really minded that we both put our careers first and each other second. Which only goes to show that what we had wasn't all that important."

"When did you stop seeing each other?"

"Just under a year ago, when Tim and I first began to discuss selling Futron. I was starting to realize then that I wanted more in my life than what I had, more than an all-consuming career and an empty, primarily physical affair. Dolores, on the other hand, was perfectly content the way she was. Last I heard, I'd been replaced by another upwardly mobile workaholic with whom she has another convenient, undemanding relationship."

He dropped a kiss on her temple, then dragged his lips lightly across her cheek to the corner of her mouth. "Now I know just how empty my relationship with Dolores was. She never made me feel the way you did on Friday. Never." He nibbled at her lower lip.

Merry's eyelids drifted downward as her mind began to fog. One last question pushed its way past her softening, trembling lips. "What are you going to do with yourself here in Springfield?"

Pulling her more fully into his arms, he continued to caress her face with his lips, his voice a warm whisper against her flushed skin. "I'm going to build a successful new business. And I'm going to dedicate myself to making one Merry James very happy. Starting now."

Even as his mouth claimed hers completely and his hands began to move demandingly over her undeniably willing body, Merry found herself wondering how long Grant would be satisfied with waiting for her to have time for him. But then he was pressing her backward, into the soft vinyl cushions of the sofa, and all intelligent thought left her.

"Ah, Merry, I've been wanting to do this all day," Grant whispered into her throat, his hand moving to the buttons of her khaki cotton safari dress. "Do you know how hard it's been for me to restrain myself in front of your friends and family?"

"You've managed very well," she murmured in response, her back arching as he found her breast with his fingers. "The—oh, Grant—the perfect gentleman."

"You don't think anyone could tell that I was lusting after you all day?" His fingers found the buckle of her heavy red belt, tugging at it even as his mouth moved lower toward her swelling breasts.

"If they could, then they surely realized that I felt the same way about you," she replied, her hands busily opening the buttons of his shirt. And she *had* felt the same way, she acknowledged to herself. All day—no, all weekend, ever since they'd parted on Friday—she'd wanted to feel Grant against her, inside her again. Needed to feel him. For someone who had gone without physical intimacy for so long, she was rapidly developing an overwhelming craving for it. But not for just anyone.

"Grant," she moaned softly. "Only Grant."

He groaned in satisfaction and impatiently divested her of her dress. It was only a matter of moments before they were both nude and Merry finally felt his full length against her once more. She sighed her delight, holding him with greedy hands. For what seemed like a long time, they were content just to lie still, faces pressed together, arms locked, legs entwined. Merry thought that she would willingly lie this way for an eternity.

But the time came when closeness wasn't enough for either of them. Grant moved, just a little, and Merry felt him hard and hot against her thigh. Her response was immediate and electric as her body demanded satisfaction. She arched beneath him, her thighs closing around his hips in sensual invitation. Grant muttered something unintelligible and surged against her, driving himself completely into her. Merry cried out in startled pleasure. And then cried out again in dismay when he withdrew and fastened his mouth to one swollen breast.

His hard, hungry suckling caused her breath to catch somewhere in the depths of her throat, effectively blocking the frustrated sounds she felt forming deep inside her. She arched again and again, trying to draw him back into her, longing for that wonderful sense of fullness that he had given her so briefly. Again he seemed willing to accede to her demands and entered her, only to pull back once more and continue with his glorious assault on her breasts.

"Grant!" she said in a gasp, her fingernails digging deep crescents into his shoulders. "Oh, Grant, *please*."

"You do want me, don't you, Merry?" he asked her, his voice raw, barely recognizable.

"Yes, oh, *yes*," she returned, almost sobbing. "I've never, never wanted anyone this much before. Please, Grant."

"Do you know what it does to me to know you want me like this?" He kissed her hard, thoroughly, before finally giving in to her pleading. This time when he entered her, he stayed, thrusting deeper and faster until she shuddered in violent release, crying his name. Once, twice more, and then Grant followed her into oblivion, groaning softly as his body tensed and then collapsed on top of her.

It took a long time for Merry to bring her breathing under control, her short, ragged pants finally easing into a more comfortable pattern. Still she clung to Grant, cradling him in her arms until his own heart rate slowed to near normal. When finally he lifted his head from her breast, he smiled tenderly at the look on her face—a look that she knew must have reflected her dazed, thunderstruck emotions. "Shell-shocked, my love?" he murmured sympathetically.

"To say the least," she replied, her throat dry. "My God, Grant."

He chuckled and shifted his weight until they were lying side by side, her head on his shoulder. "Any more questions about whether I'll be leaving Springfield?"

Her head lifted abruptly, almost clipping him under the chin. "You were trying to prove a point?" she demanded.

"No, love," he assured her, pulling her head back down to his damp shoulder. "I wasn't trying to prove anything. What happened between us was simply a matter of spontaneous combustion."

"Humph." Merry squirmed against him, remembering the way he had tormented her until she'd begged for him. Oddly enough, she wasn't annoyed with him. After all, he had just taken her to even greater heights of sensual pleasure than he had the first time they'd made love, and she hadn't honestly believed that was possible.

"Keep wiggling against me, sweetheart, and you're going to get me started all over again," Grant warned her.

Merry laughed softly. "A bit overconfident, aren't we?"

"You think so?" He shifted suddenly, lifting her over him until she sprawled across his chest. He raised his hips just enough for her to feel his growing arousal, then chuckled when her eyes widened appreciatively. "What do you say about my confidence now?"

She rubbed one of his hair-roughened legs with the sole of her foot as she nibbled at his lower lip. "I say I should never have doubted you."

"Damned straight. Now that you've put me in this condition, what are you going to do about it?" he asked challengingly.

"Gee, I don't know. Got any ideas?"

"Honey, I've had ideas ever since I walked into your office the other day and saw that saddle on your desk," he teased.

Merry eyed him suspiciously. "I'm not sure I even want to know what you'd do with that saddle. Maybe I'd better come up with some ideas of my own."

"Be my guest."

"I could start out by doing something like this."

He cleared his throat and arched into her hands. "Yes, you could start out that way."

"And then I could try a bit of this."

"Ye-es." The word broke in the middle as Grant's eyes drifted closed.

"And maybe—"

"Oh, God, Merry. Don't stop now."

IT WAS QUITE LATE when Grant dropped Merry off at her house. "I wish I could spend the night with you," he murmured against her lips as he kissed her good-night on the porch. "I want to wake up with you in the morning, to make love with you when you're still flushed and dreamy from sleep."

Merry's heart turned over at the image of waking in Grant's arms, but she didn't bother to tell him that she, too, would like that very much. She decided that things had gone quite far enough between them for one evening. "Good night, Grant," she told him softly.

"Good night, Merry. I'll call you tomorrow."

"All right." She reached for the doorknob, watching him walk away. He had just stepped off the porch when his name left her lips, seemingly of its own volition. "Grant . . ."

He looked back. "Yes, love?"

What could she say? *It was wonderful? Thank you for making me feel more like a woman than I've ever felt before? I love you?* "Good night, Grant," she said at last.

"Good night, Merry," he told her again, smiling as if he understood. And then he was gone.

6

MARSHA WAS WAITING on Merry's bed, clad in nightgown and robe, a book resting on her knees. "I was about to give up on you."

"You should have. It's very late."

"Mmm. I take it Grant no longer makes you nervous?"

Merry sighed, tossing her purse onto a rocking chair and beginning to unbutton her dress. "He terrifies me." She shrugged out of her dress.

Marsha laughed softly. "Well, at least you've stopped running."

Merry gave her sister a wry look as she dug a nightgown out of a bureau drawer. "Believe me, Marsha, with Grant I have no choice. The man does not know how to accept refusal."

"I like him, Merry."

Merry stroked her lower lip with one finger, then roused herself enough to tug on her gown. "So do I," she said at last.

"It's more than liking in your case, I think."

"Marsha, I've only known him for a few days."

"Does that matter?"

Combing her fingers through her hair, Merry shook her head ruefully. "No, I suppose not." She paused before continuing. "Grant . . . he and I . . ."

"I know."

"I should have known you would." Merry sank onto the bed and wrapped her arms around her bent legs, her chin resting on her knees. "Lord, I'm tired."

"You really are still scared, aren't you?" Marsha asked perceptively, placing her book on the nightstand beside the bed and turning to face her sister. "Are you so afraid of being hurt again?"

"Again?" Merry closed her eyes briefly and gave a short laugh that contained no humor. "As if...whatever this is between me and Grant could ever compare to the way I felt about Justin. Justin never frightened me like this, Marsha."

"I've always heard real love is like that," Marsha mused. "Terrifying. Doesn't sound like the stuff they sing of in love songs, does it?"

"I don't even know if this *is* love," Merry grumbled, knowing she sounded cross but unable to help herself. "It's happening too fast, too intensely. A week ago I didn't even know Grant existed, and now...now everything has changed."

"Change isn't always bad, Merry. Sometimes things change because it's time."

Merry groaned and flopped onto her pillow. "Let's not get philosophical tonight, Marsh. I just don't think I'm up to it."

"You do look tired," Marsha observed, frowning thoughtfully at the dark circles that Merry knew must have been under her eyes. "I guess it was quite a date."

"Go away, Marsha."

Marsha struggled to hide a grin. "So where did he take you, anyway? A motel? Hardly a good example for your innocent little sisters, Merry Kathleen."

"We didn't go to a motel! We went to—" Merry stopped, grimaced, then laughed reluctantly. "We went to the office. Now will you *please* go away and let me get some sleep?"

"Gave at the office, huh? Seems like I've heard that one before." With that flip comment Marsha turned out the light and left for her own room.

Muttering about little sisters, whatever their ages, Merry pulled the covers to her ears and gave in to exhaustion. She dreamed again that night, but this time her dreams were strange and surreal, leaving her disoriented and confused when she awoke the next morning. All she could remember about them was that the other people in her dreams had seemed to move past her in double time while she had moved in slow motion, trying and failing to keep up.

"HOW ABOUT TAKING some time off this afternoon to help me look for a place to live?"

Merry shook her head, then, realizing that Grant couldn't see her since he was on the other side of Springfield, spoke into the telephone receiver cradled against her shoulder. "Sorry, Grant. I couldn't possibly take off today. I have two appointments this afternoon."

"Can't Marsha handle them?"

Merry frowned as she signed her name at the bottom of a letter Marsha had just slipped across the desk. "No, Marsha is too busy trying to catch up from last week. Though, thanks to you, she's not as far behind as she might have been."

Grant's disappointed sigh was audible over the telephone, but he gave in without further argument. "Okay, I understand. Guess I'll look around a bit myself. Any suggestions?"

"You might try the new apartment complex over on Ingram Mill. They're very nice."

"I'm not looking for an apartment. I'm looking for a house."

Merry's eyebrows shot up. "Oh. I didn't realize."

"That's why I want you to help me look around. But I'll scout out a few and you can take a look when you find some time; how does that sound?"

"Of course. I'd be . . . glad to, Grant."

"So how about lunch? Got time to have lunch with me?"

She really didn't, but she was reluctant to turn him down again. "Okay, but it'll have to be a short one. I hope you understand."

"All too well, love. See you at noon."

He didn't give her time to ask him to clarify his cryptic statement. Merry stared at the phone for a moment, then replaced it in its cradle with a sigh. "Grant wanted you to go apartment hunting with him this afternoon?" Marsha asked interestedly from the other side of Merry's desk. They had been going over their calendar for the remainder of the month when Grant had called at just after ten.

"House hunting," Merry corrected, moistening lips that suddenly seemed dry.

Marsha tilted her head in avid interest. "Oh. House hunting, huh? Sounds serious."

"So maybe he just prefers houses to apartments," Merry suggested feebly.

"Does he own a house in Colorado?"

Shuffling the papers in front of her, Merry avoided her sister's laughing eyes. "Well, no, actually I think he said he lived in an apartment there."

"Uh-huh."

"What's that supposed to mean?"

Marsha feigned innocence. "Nothing."

"Marsha, Grant's choosing to look for a house rather than an apartment has nothing to do with me."

"Uh-huh," Marsha murmured with a solemn nod.

"Don't you have some work to do?" Merry demanded in frustration.

Marsha laughed. "We were doing it together, remember?"

"Oh. Right. So let's get back to it."

"Yes, boss."

"And don't call me boss!"

Marsha wisely refrained from comment, turning her attention to the calendar before her.

Merry chewed her lower lip as she tried to concentrate on her business. Unfortunately, she could think of little but Grant. Was he already starting to make demands on her time? she wondered bleakly, thinking of his casual suggestion that she take the afternoon off. Hadn't he just promised on Friday that he wouldn't complain about her other obligations? She might have agreed to go with him if he'd said he wanted to look for a house later, after she closed the office, but he had asked her to take time away from her work.

And why had he suddenly decided he needed a house, anyway? What was wrong with an apartment for a bachelor? Unless he was already planning to do something about his bachelor status. She knew he didn't believe in wasting time.

She gulped and reached for a pencil, fighting down a surge of pure panic.

At twenty minutes to twelve Melinda called from school, distraught because she'd just realized she'd left an important homework assignment at home. The paper was due to be turned in at twelve-thirty. Marsha had already left for lunch, having several business-related errands to run while she was gone, so Merry had to switch on the answering machine, close the office, stop at home, retrieve the paper from Melinda's bedroom and rush it to the school. She quickly lectured Melinda that an eighth-grader should be more responsible, and mildly threatened her sister with unpleasant consequences if such a thing happened again.

It was ten minutes after twelve when she pulled into the lot to find Grant waiting by the locked door of the office. He looked windblown, sexy and slightly annoyed. "I'm sorry, Grant. Melinda forgot her homework, and I had to go home and get it, then take it to her," she apologized immediately.

Grant frowned. "You went after Melinda's homework?" he repeated.

She shrugged, straightening her bright green skirt, which was being whipped around her legs by a brisk spring breeze. "Yes. I told her I wouldn't bail her out next time."

Grant started to say something, stopped, then leaned over to kiss her. "Hi."

She smiled brightly, relieved that a potentially tense moment seemed to have passed. "Hi."

"Ready to go to lunch?"

"Sure. Let's go."

Announcing that he was in the mood for Chinese food, Grant took Merry to Gee's East Wind Restaurant. She crossed her fingers, hoping that service would be especially quick that day, ordering the lunch special.

"I drove around for a while this morning after I talked to you," Grant told her between bites of his cashew chicken. "There are several nice homes for sale, particularly in the Brentwood, Cinnamon Square and Cooper Estates divisions."

"Yes, those are all nice areas," Merry agreed, pushing her sweet-and-sour pork around on her plate. She wasn't sure that she was ready to discuss houses with Grant.

Oblivious to her reluctance, he pressed on. "What do you think of Cinnamon Square?"

"It's very nice."

"I thought so, too. There was one house, especially, that caught my eye. Maybe I could make an appointment for us to see it one afternoon this week—whenever you have time," he added carefully.

Nodding, Merry took a bite of her lunch. When she'd swallowed, she couldn't resist asking, "What's your hurry to find a house?"

Grant shrugged. "I've already been at Leida's almost two weeks. She doesn't mind, but it's time I started looking for my own place. It may take some time to find exactly what we—what I want, and in the meantime I'm paying rent on an apartment in Colorado that's not being used."

Choosing to ignore his verbal stumble, Merry decided to change the subject. For the next few minutes they talked about some of the upcoming parties on her calendar. She had told him before that spring was her busiest season, her schedule filled with a number of proms, debuts and wedding receptions that she was arranging. As the reputation of MerryMakers spread, she was receiving more and more calls from surrounding towns—Republic, Ozark, Marshfield, even Joplin, which was about seventy miles away.

"People like the way we work with them to stay within their price range. We'll do as much or as little of the actual party as they want." Merry was aware that she was chattering about things Grant already knew, but at least she was on safe ground with her business.

"You may have to hire more employees—full-time employees," he elaborated. "And you should look into computerizing. It would make your scheduling and billing a lot easier."

Merry grimaced. "I don't know much about computers," she admitted. "Before Marsha and I started MerryMakers with the money we inherited from our parents, I worked for the Convention and Visitors' Bureau here in Springfield. I didn't really use the computers there much. I took one data processing course in the business college I attended after high school, but I wouldn't have the least idea how to program a computer for our particular business needs, and computer consultants are so expensive that I haven't been able to justify the expense yet."

Grant smiled encouragingly, filing her words away in his mind. This was just the type of business owner he was interested in dealing with, he thought. Those who still viewed computers as the domain of big business and genius-level operators. Not ready to go into the details of a business he hadn't even started yet, he said simply, "I just happen to know a bit about the subject. I'll teach you."

"I'll think about it," she answered vaguely, wondering again what Grant's business plans were. How long would it be before he grew bored with having nothing to do? A man who had built a successful company from scratch and managed it for thirteen years would not be happy for long doing nothing. She wondered how much of his sudden interest in her was the result of the challenge of pursuit. Not that she proved to be much of a challenge.

"You're being awfully quiet all of a sudden," Grant observed, watching her closely. "Is something wrong?"

"No," she answered, forcing a smile. "It's just that I really have to get back to work now."

Seeming to accept her answer, he reached for the check.

GRANT ACCOMPANIED Merry inside when they returned to her office, pausing to speak to Marsha at the reception desk. He was teasing Marsha about her filing system when the outer door opened and two men walked in—a portly, middle-aged man whose uniform proclaimed him to be sheriff of Greene County and a younger, darkly tanned man in an inexpensive brown suit. Something about their expression told Grant that they were not there to make arrangements for a party. He decided to hang around for a while.

"May I help you?" Marsha asked politely, her gray eyes wide with curiosity.

"I'm Sheriff Roland and this is Detective Litchfield. We'd like to speak to Merry James," the older man announced.

"I'm Merry James," Merry told him, with a brief, quizzical look at her sister. "What can I do for you?"

"We'd like to ask you some questions, ma'am. Perhaps we could go into your office?"

"Yes, of course." Merry gestured toward the open door behind the reception desk. Grant took a protective step toward Merry, not liking the look on the younger cop's face. Litchfield had been watching Merry with an odd combination of speculative interest and suspicion. "Is there a problem, officers?"

Aware of Merry's startled—and not altogether pleased—expression, Grant waited implacably for an answer to his question.

"And you are...?" Roland inquired blandly, his faded blue eyes trained intently on Grant.

"Grant Bryant."

"And what is your relationship with Miss James?" Roland asked, still without expression.

"A very close one," Grant returned with equal aplomb, though he winced mentally at Merry's probable reaction later. He had done nothing more than tell the truth, he told himself reassuringly, but Merry would probably tear a few wide strips off him for butting in.

"Is that right?" Roland lifted a gray eyebrow at the embarrassed expression on Merry's face, then looked back at Grant with a twist of his mouth that somewhat resembled a smile. "You're welcome to join us in Miss James's office, Mr. Bryant."

"Thank you, Sheriff." Grant took Merry's arm without quite meeting her eyes and discreetly nudged her in the direction of her office.

The sheriff waited until Merry was seated behind her desk, Grant leaning on the credenza behind her, and Litchfield and himself in chairs facing them before beginning his questioning. "You own this business, don't you, Miss James?"

"My sister and I own it, though I am listed as president," Merry replied.

"How long have you been in business?"

"A year. What's this all about, Sheriff?"

He told her, giving only clipped concise facts. There had been a recent rash of home robberies in the area. All of the victims were away for a few hours when their homes were robbed. The police had noticed another interesting pattern—most of the victims had been attending functions organized by MerryMakers at the times of the robberies.

Grant scowled. "You think MerryMakers is connected to these crimes?" he demanded.

"Surely not," Merry said defensively.

"You gotta admit it looks suspicious," Litchfield put in, the first time he had spoken since he'd arrived.

"Do you have lists of the guests who will be attending your parties, Miss James?" Sheriff Roland inquired mildly, flicking a warning look at the detective.

"Most of the time we do. That's how we know how many people to plan for, or make place cards or name tags for, if necessary. We also need the names for the newspaper, when applicable, or the photographer who works many of our parties to provide souvenir photos for the guests."

"So this photographer has access to the guest list. Who else?"

"The lists are kept in the files with all the pertinent material for each event. I suppose any of my employees would have limited access to the files. There's only Marsha and me and four part-time employees. Oh, and my younger sisters help us out after school."

Roland only nodded and opened a notebook, holding a pencil above it. "Please give me the names of your employees."

Merry looked nervously at Grant. Concerned with the loss of color in her cheeks, he placed a reassuring hand on her shoulder. As if finding some measure of strength in his touch, Merry turned back to the sheriff. "Linda Patterson, a homemaker who works part-time with us to make extra money, and three college students—Kirk Mitchell and Anne Baker attend Southwest Missouri State U. and Louis Webster goes to Drury College. They usually help at the site of the party, setting up, serving or cleaning up afterward. There's really no reason for any of them to go into the files, except on occasion when I've requested them to do so for some reason."

"But they do have access to the files?"

Merry shrugged slightly. "I suppose it's possible that any of them could get into the files without Marsha or me noticing, but it's not probable. I've known most of my employees for some time, Sheriff. They're are all fine young people and completely trustworthy. I wouldn't have hired them otherwise."

"What about your sisters? They hang around much?"

"They help out after school, as I said. But they—"

"Their names, please."

Grant tightened his fingers on Merry's shoulder as he felt her stir in agitation. He had a feeling that his gentle love would quickly lose her temper if the blunt sheriff continued to make implications about her family. Grant was holding on to his own temper and patience with an effort.

"Melinda and Meaghan. They're only in the eighth grade."

"The girls have boyfriends?"

Merry lifted her chin. "Why do you ask?" Grant could tell that she was rapidly reaching the limit of patience.

Litchfield spoke up again. "We heard one of your sisters is dating that Taylor kid. The boy who dresses like a punk rocker and stays in trouble most of the time."

"So you've already been asking around about us?" Merry asked indignantly. "Do you know what that can do to our business?"

"I assure you we are being very discreet in our investigation, Miss James," Roland said with another look at the detective. "Is it true that one of your sisters is dating the Taylor boy?"

"Yes," Merry answered reluctantly. "Melinda has been seeing Savage. And if you'll check your records, you'll notice that he hasn't been in any trouble in several months—not since he met Melinda," she added with a touch of defiance.

"And what about you, Mr. Bryant?" Litchfield demanded. "What do you do?"

"I'm between jobs right now," Grant answered smoothly, leaning comfortably against the credenza. He only smiled when Merry gave him a reproving frown. He saw no reason at this point to defend himself to this man by explaining his recent career move.

"Is that right? You from Missouri?"

"No, until recently I lived in Colorado."

"How long you been here?" Litchfield continued suspiciously.

"A couple of weeks."

"And how long have you known Miss James?"

"Not very long."

Litchfield cocked his head. "But you already have a 'very close' relationship with her?" he inquired snidely, mimicking Grant's earlier words.

"Hmm," Grant murmured affirmatively. He winked at Merry. "I don't believe in wasting time, you see." He was pleased when Merry's lips twitched in a near smile.

"Excuse me, Merry." Marsha spoke from the doorway, her expression anxious. Since they hadn't bothered to close the door between the offices, Grant assumed that Marsha had heard most of the conversation. "Ms Kropf is here for her appointment to discuss the Jaycees banquet."

"We won't keep you away from your work any longer, Miss James," Roland said, shoving his heavy frame out of the undersize chair he'd taken. "And we have other people to see this afternoon. We'll get back to you when we have further questions."

"And they *will* have further questions," Grant murmured when the two police officers had departed.

"They really didn't ask very many this time, did they?" Merry whispered worriedly, conscious of the woman waiting in the reception area to see her. "Why didn't they ask about . . . about alibis, and motives, and other crime stuff?"

Grant chuckled. "You've been watching too much television, love. They'll do some more investigating with what you gave them today, and then they'll be back with more specific questions for you. I think the purpose of today's visit was just to make contact. At this time they obviously don't have very much to connect Merry-Makers with the robberies."

"If this gets out, it could really damage our reputation." Merry moistened her lips in anxiety, drawing Grant's eyes to them and reminding him that it had been hours since he'd really been alone with her. He wanted nothing more at this moment than to hold her and assure her that everything would be all right, but he, too, was conscious of their surroundings and her obligations.

"Take care of your appointment, Merry," he told her quietly. "I'll get out of your way. I'll call you later, okay?"

Her eyes suddenly narrowed at him. "Yes, you and I *do* have a few things to discuss, Grant Bryant. Why did you tell those—"

Grant pressed a hard kiss on her mouth to postpone that particular question, ruthlessly controlling his need to take her in his arms and hold her there. "I'll call you later," he promised again when he pulled away, then walked out without giving her a chance to reply. He nodded politely to the attractive young woman who entered Merry's office as he left, noting that Merry's voice was admirably normal when she greeted her customer.

"Grant, do you really think the police suspect us of having anything to do with those robberies?" Marsha whispered anxiously, catching his arm and confirming his surmise that she'd heard most of the conversation. Sheriff Roland would have known that Marsha could hear; he would have closed the office door if he cared. Grant wondered if the sharp-eyed sheriff had been deliberately casual with the brief visit, hoping to confuse Merry or Marsha into admitting whether they knew anything about the robberies.

He walked with Marsha to the door, then lowered his voice so that there would be no possibility of being overheard by the woman in Merry's office. "Any chance at all that one of your employees could be involved in this?"

Marsha shook her silvery-blond head emphatically. "I can't believe that. Linda is one of the sweetest people I know, and the others are all nice, clean-cut types who work for us to earn a little extra money while they attend college."

"What about Savage? The cops said he'd been in a lot of trouble in the past."

Marsha frowned. "Well, not a lot of trouble. Some. He has a hot temper, you see, and he tends to lose it when guys make derogatory comments about his appearance or his family. His mother left home several years ago and his father's a little strange, so sometimes other kids taunt him."

"No history of theft?"

"Not that I'm aware of," she answered flatly. "Merry and I would never allow Melinda to see him if we thought he was really a bad boy."

"Matt's not too pleased about Melinda's seeing him," Grant reminded her.

Marsha gave him a faint smile. "Matt's overprotective," she explained. "He thinks Melinda is too young to have a boyfriend at all. Savage's age and history don't help."

Grant nodded his understanding. "I'll go now and let you get back to work. I'll be back later. Try not to worry, okay?"

"I'll try. Grant?"

"Yes, Marsha?"

"Merry's going to yell at you for telling the sheriff that you're involved with her, you know. She won't think it's any of his business."

He grinned. "At least I didn't introduce myself as her fiancé. That was my first instinct."

She eyed him speculatively. "Was it?"

"Yep." He grinned, winked at her and then left.

MERRY HAD A HEADACHE. A bad one. And it was growing worse by the minute. The day had started out badly enough, but it had steadily deteriorated ever since the sheriff and the unpleasant Detective Litchfield had left her office. She'd informed the twins exactly what the sheriff had told her, as well as each question he'd asked. She'd deliberated about how much to tell them but had decided they might as well know the whole truth. Now she was wondering if she'd made the right decision.

"I can't believe he'd think anyone associated with MerryMakers had anything to do with those robberies!" Meaghan muttered in disgust. "What a jerk."

"It's not fair that Savage always gets blamed for everything just because he doesn't look or dress like everyone else," Melinda complained vociferously. "Savage would never rob anyone. He has too much integrity."

"Nobody connected with MerryMakers would rob anyone," Meaghan agreed heatedly. "How could anyone suspect us or Linda, or Kirk, or Louis—or even Boyd or Savage, just because they're our boyfriends! It's stupid."

"Sheriff Roland didn't actually accuse anyone," Merry felt compelled to point out. "He just noticed that several of the victims were attending functions we organized when their houses were robbed. He's only doing his job to follow up on that."

"I really don't think we should say anything about this outside of the office or home," Marsha suggested cautiously. "We can't let word of this get out."

"As if we could stop it." Meaghan looked concerned as she realized for the first time the kind of effect such gossip could have on the business her sisters had invested so much in.

"Marsha's right," Merry said. "Let's keep it quiet, okay?"

Melinda pushed her strawberry-blond hair out of her sober face and looked at her oldest sister with concern. "Merry, Savage didn't have anything to do with this. I swear it!"

"You don't have to swear, honey, I know he didn't." Merry smiled reassuringly at her little sister. "Savage doesn't sneak around. He falls into trouble right out in the open where everyone can see."

Relieved, Melinda giggled. "You got that right."

"Is this a private conference or can anyone sit in?" Grant's deep voice brought everyone's attention around to the door of Merry's office, where her sisters had gathered.

"Does he know?" Melinda asked in an audible whisper.

"He knows," Merry answered, trying to control her suddenly erratic heart rate by reminding herself that she was still furious with the undeniably attractive man in her doorway. She pulled her gaze away from him and glanced down at her watch. "It's after five. You kids can leave if you want."

"Go on out to the car, girls," Marsha told them. "I'll be there in just a minute."

Grant slipped an arm around Merry's shoulders. "Rough day, wasn't it, love?"

"Yes, it was," Merry retorted resentfully, rubbing her throbbing temples. "And you didn't make it any easier. You want to tell me why you told Sheriff Roland and Detective Litchfield that we have a 'very close' relationship? You made it sound like we were engaged, or involved in a torrid love affair, at the least."

"I wanted to find out what was going on," he answered, pushing her hands aside to take over the soothing massage. "Besides, we *do* have a very close relationship. At the least."

Fighting an insane urge to purr beneath the gentle movements of his fingers at her temples, Merry tried to retain her grip on reality. "You, Grant Bryant, are a very strange man."

She knew he was grinning, though her eyelids had drifted shut. "So I've been told."

Marsha laughed, abruptly reminding Merry that she and Grant were not alone. Her lids opened, and she found her gaze was locked with Grant's. The expression in his light blue eyes made her knees go weak. It really wasn't fair that he should be able to do this to her with only a look, she thought dazedly.

"As much as I'm enjoying this snappy repartee, I'm beginning to feel a bit superfluous," Marsha said teasingly. "I think I'll go home now. Can I assume that you're driving Merry home, Grant?"

"Yes. We'll be there in a few minutes. I don't think Merry is in the mood to go out tonight."

Merry cleared her throat. "Why doesn't anyone ask me what I plan to do? You're talking about me like I'm not even in the room."

"Sorry, love." Grant dropped a kiss on her forehead and stepped back. "May I please drive you home?"

"Yes, Grant. Take me home."

7

MERRY WAS RATHER QUIET during the drive home, but
Grant did not push her into conversation. Instead, he
turned the radio to a soft rock station, seemingly content just to be with her. "Would you like to join us for
dinner?" she roused herself to ask when he stopped the
car in front of her house. "We're having pot roast."

Grant seemed about to accept, then he paused, looked
at her closely for a moment and shook his head. "No, not
tonight. But thank you for asking."

Unexpectedly disappointed, Merry tilted her head in-
quiringly at him. "You really are welcome to stay."

"Not tonight," he said again gently, knowing she
needed some time alone to deal with this latest complication in her already complicated life. He ached for her,
wanted very much to help her, but all he could think of
to do now was to give her a bit of space. "I'd like to see
you tomorrow night. Are you free?"

"Yes—no, tomorrow night is Tuesday. I have a class."

"A class?" he asked swiftly. "What kind of class?"

She cleared her throat a bit self-consciously. "Guitar
class."

"Guitar? Really? How long have you been playing?"
He seemed genuinely interested.

"I've been taking classes one night a week since Sep-
tember," she explained. "It was something I always
wanted to do, but I just never got around to it until recently."

"Are you any good?"

She shrugged. "I'd never make a professional musician, but that's not what I wanted, anyway. I just wanted to know how to play."

"I see." He draped an arm around her shoulders and pulled her across the console to kiss her. "I think it's nice that you're doing something you want to do."

"I told you I do things just for myself sometimes," she reminded him, her hands going almost unconsciously to his shoulders.

He nibbled at her lower lip. "You'll have to play for me sometime."

She closed her eyes and leaned farther toward him. "Maybe I will," she whispered, tilting her head back in invitation.

Grant kissed her, and then kissed her again and again, each time more deeply, more passionately than before. Forgetting her headache, her problems, their surroundings, Merry wrapped her arms around Grant's neck and returned the kisses just as fervently. It seemed as if days had passed since she'd kissed him like this, not just the night before.

"Merry." Grant's voice was a husky whisper.

She ignored him, seeking his lips again.

He held her off, though she felt the fine tremor in the hands he placed on her shoulders. "Merry."

She sighed and opened her eyes. "What?"

"There are two giggling teenagers watching us from your living-room window."

Merry's eyes closed again briefly as she groaned in embarrassment. "Oh, no."

"Oh, yes. Much as I'd love to continue this, I'm not sure those two need any new ideas."

"You're right." She pulled away from him reluctantly. "Are you sure you won't stay for dinner?"

"Honey, if I walk in that house in this condition, you're really going to be embarrassed," Grant told her ruefully, glancing pointedly down at his lap.

Merry blushed vividly. "Oh."

"Yes, oh. I'll call you later, okay?"

She nodded and climbed out of the car, glaring ominously at the oversize living-room window, where two strawberry-blond heads ducked out of sight immediately. "I think I'll go have a talk with the twins," she muttered just before she closed the car door.

"Go easy on my future sisters-in-law," Grant quipped just as the door shut. Before Merry could open the door again to respond to his incredible audacity, he was backing the car out of the drive. Glaring at the impudently red vehicle, Merry decided to take her annoyance out on two available targets.

"Melinda! Meaghan!"

Several hours and three Extra-Strength Tylenol later, Merry lay in bed staring at her darkened ceiling and wondered what was bothering her more—Matt's leaving in a few days, the police investigation concerning her business or Grant's relentless pursuit. Grant was the one who remained prominent in her thoughts. What had he meant by that crack about his future sisters-in-law? Did he really intend to marry her? On the basis of less than a week's acquaintance, one dinner date and making love twice? Or was he only teasing her, trying to make her laugh and forget about her problems for a while? One could never tell with Grant.

Ruthlessly examining her own feelings, she realized that it would be all too easy for her to start fantasizing about marriage to Grant. He was already an important part of her life, threatening the protective shields she'd tried to erect against him. Unfortunately, she could not afford to be that trusting. Maybe he thought he wanted to marry her now, but she could think of many reasons he could be deluding himself. Boredom, challenge, lust, infatuation, all combined into a maelstrom of emotion that he might mistake for love. How could he love her? He barely knew her.

Of course, she loved him with all her heart—probably had from about five minutes after meeting him—but that was different. Merry had been in love before, though not to this extent. She knew how to recognize the emotion. Grant, on the other hand, had told her that he had little or no experience with love. He'd been too immersed in his business to allow himself more than a dreadful-sounding affair with that Dolores person, a woman who hadn't had the sense to recognize a good thing when she'd had it. How could any woman, having been intimate with Grant, ever walk away from him?

Merry knew that she could not. Nor could she watch him walk away without having a portion of her heart leave with him. And that was why she was lying here in a cold sweat, desperately wishing there was a way to know if what Grant professed to feel for her was real.

Didn't he know the drawbacks of becoming involved with a woman with her responsibilities? It wasn't just her career—he'd dated other career women. But if this investigation continued, or grew worse, Merry might find herself struggling for survival, businesswise. Lord only knew what that would entail.

And she was responsible for two teenagers. Sure, Marsha helped out a great deal with the twins, but Merry was their legal guardian, ultimately responsible for their health and welfare. The twins would be in school for four

more years before entering college. Merry was facing all
the responsibilities of a parent—worrying about grades,
curfews, sex, drug use, car accidents—all those other
adolescent horrors that preyed on her mind during the
wee hours of some nights.

Somehow she had to find a way to make Grant aware
of their problems and to find out if he was willing to take
on those problems. It was a simple matter of self-
preservation.

GRANT CALLED THE OFFICE early Tuesday morning, and
Merry started what she called her "open-his-eyes-
campaign" immediately. When he asked her for lunch,
she turned him down—legitimately, as it turned out. "I
can't, Grant. I'm having lunch with a client. She's host-
ing a luncheon at her home tomorrow, and we're going
over last-minute details today."

"So that means you'll be tied up for lunch tomorrow,
as well?"

"I'm afraid so."

"I know you have your guitar class tonight. Will I see
you tomorrow night?"

"No, we have a party tomorrow night."

"Come on, Merry," he said impatiently. "When can I
see you?"

"I don't know, Grant. Why don't you let me call you
when I have time?" she suggested, nervously moistening her lips.

"Call me when you have time?" Grant repeated in an
ominously quiet voice.

"Grant, I've told you this is a busy time for me. This
whole week is full. I'll see you at Leida's party Saturday,
and I have a couple of free nights next week—"

"Dammit, Merry, you're not even trying! You're running from me again, aren't you?" Grant's anger came through the receiver quite clearly.

The slightest niggling of a guilty conscience fed Merry's own temper. "I'm not running! But you're pushing, just as I knew you would. You promised that you wouldn't pressure me, that you'd understand my other obligations."

"Within reason, yes."

"The problem with you, Grant," she continued as if he hadn't spoken, "is that you're bored. It was boredom that had you working for me last week, and now you don't even have that. What are you planning to do with your days, Grant, sit around and watch the soaps? Stay on the phone with me? You are much too active a person to be content with this life of leisure for very long, and I'm afraid I just don't have time to serve as your primary form of entertainment!"

She immediately wished she hadn't phrased that last sentence quite that way, but it was too late to soften her words. She waited rather anxiously for Grant's response.

When it came, she knew he was coldly furious. "That attack was uncalled for, Merry. I only asked to see you. And as far as giving you time, why do you think I didn't hang around last night? I knew you had a lot on your mind after your talk with the sheriff."

"Look, Grant, I'm sorry—"

"Contrary to what you may believe, I do have plans for my future, Merry. I suppose I should have told you about them, but then, you've never made much of an effort to find out. I know you have a lot to deal with now, and I want to help you, but not by serving as the target for your anger. I'll be a sounding board, or a refuge if you wish, but I won't be a whipping boy!" And with that he hung up.

"Damn." Merry slammed down the receiver, knowing she had handled the call all wrong. Grant was right, she thought bleakly. She *had* taken her frustrations and fears out on him. She didn't blame him for being annoyed with her, but she wondered if he would give up on her that easily. She truly hoped he would not.

"What's wrong?" Marsha asked, appearing in the doorway, a splash of color in her bright pink sweater and skirt.

Not particularly cheered by her sister's vivid attire, Merry decided her own black dress with its discreet touches of white at the collar and cuff more closely suited her mood. "Grant and I had a disagreement," she answered glumly.

"A fight, you mean?" Marsha asked with interested curiosity brightening her gray eyes.

"A quarrel," Merry qualified, grimacing.

"Serious?"

"I don't know yet."

Marsha leaned against the doorframe and eyed her sister with a quizzical smile. "Has it occurred to you, Merry, that you and Grant seem to have skipped a few steps somewhere? I mean, you really just met the guy a week ago tomorrow and already you're having your first lover's quarrel."

"Yeah. It's occurred to me," Merry agreed dryly. "Somehow we've ignored the formalities—like an introduction, a first date and then a couple of months' worth of other dates before anything serious develops. And Grant wonders why I'm feeling pressured."

"I can't imagine why you'd feel pressured," Marsha quipped, obviously trying to tease her sister into a better humor. "Just because the man's already practically become a member of the family..."

"That's why." Merry's mouth quirked into one of her tilted smiles, despite herself. "How do I get myself into these situations, Marsha?"

"I only wish someone like Grant would come along and fall immediately in love with me," Marsha responded. "You're complaining about being swept off your feet by a gorgeous—and, I might add, financially solvent—man with beautiful blue eyes and a romantic nature, while I'm spending my free evenings fighting off passes from overdeveloped, underdeveloped Neanderthals."

"Overdeveloped, underdeveloped?"

Marsha nodded emphatically. "Overdeveloped physically, underdeveloped mentally."

"Ah, we're talking about Bruce Nelson, the former pride of the Aggies football team, now running his father's manufacturing company," Merry teased.

"That's the one. And the really sad part is, he's been the best of the lot lately. I don't suppose Leida has another brother hidden somewhere?"

"No. But I think Grant's former business partner is available." Merry's smile dimmed as she was assailed by doubts about her own unusual romance.

Perceptive as usual, Marsha came forward to pat her sister's shoulder. "Don't worry about it, Merry. It will work out. Grant's crazy about you. Give him a chance, will you?"

Merry shook her head when Marsha would have spoken further. "Let's not talk about it anymore right now, okay? I have to get ready for my lunch with Betty Anderson. Do you have any Tylenol in your desk?"

"I think so. Got another headache?"

"Yes. Tension, I guess. I'll try not to worry about things so much."

"Good. You're not alone, you know. You've got your family, and your friends, and you have Grant if you'll quit pushing him away. I know," Marsha said hastily, holding both hands up in a conciliatory gesture. "You don't want to talk about it. I'll go get the Tylenol."

"Thank you." Merry shoved a stray lock of dark hair off her aching forehead and reached for the Anderson file.

"SO HOW IS PARADISE?" Grant inquired of the man talking to him on the telephone.

"I hate to admit it, buddy, but you were right," Tim replied. "I'm bored. Boy, am I bored!"

Grant chuckled and reclined more comfortably against the cushions of his sister's den sofa. "Good thing I'm not the type to say I told you so."

"So why do I get the feeling that you just said it?" Without waiting for a reply to his whimsical question, Tim continued. "How are things in Missouri?"

"Interesting. Stimulating. Frustrating."

There was a pause, and then, "You want to explain that?"

"I've met someone."

"A woman?"

Grant twisted his mouth into a wry grin. "What do you think?"

"I think if you were interested in men, I'd have known it by now. Who is she?"

"Her name is Merry James. She has brown hair, green eyes, a beautiful smile and a temper."

Tim laughed. "Sounds intriguing."

"I'm in love with her. I'm going to marry her."

The ensuing silence was so long that Grant cleared his throat. "Tim?"

"I heard you. I just had to pick myself up off the ground. You say you're getting married?"

"Yes."

"Does the lady know it?"

"She's resisting a bit, but I'm pretty sure she knows."

"Ask Leida if her offer of room and board is still open. I suddenly feel the urge to visit Missouri."

"Something told me you might." Grant idly twisted the telephone cord around his index finger, staring at it as he spoke. "I was hoping you would, actually."

"Problems?"

"A few." He briefly outlined Merry's confrontation with the local police.

"Hmm. Got any ideas?"

"Maybe. I've got some ideas about a new business, too," he said, glancing at the stacks of papers at his elbow—the business proposal he'd been putting together for the past few days. He hadn't mentioned the hours of work to Merry, but then he shouldn't have to explain to her that he had other things to do than be entertained by her, he thought somewhat resentfully. "You interested in hearing them?"

"Hell, yes, I'm interested. I'm just not cut out for a life of leisure."

Grant winced. "I've recently been informed that I'm not, either."

"Merry?"

"Yeah. She told me to find something to do with myself other than chase after her."

Tim laughed heartily. "I think I'm going to like this lady. She wouldn't have a sister, would she?"

"Three of them. All beautiful blondes."

"I'll be there tomorrow."

"Great. Let me know when you're arriving and I'll pick you up at the airport."

"All right! Castle and Bryant, together again. Think Springfield's ready for us?"

"Guess we'll find out, won't we? See you tomorrow, buddy." Grant was grinning for the first time since his argument with Merry, when he hung up the phone. Tim's call had done wonders for his mood. He was feeling terribly guilty for quarrelling with her when she already had so much to deal with. It took him another half hour to admit to himself that she might have had reason to worry that he had nothing to do with himself except pursue her. After all, he hadn't told her about the business ideas he'd been working on. No wonder she was feeling pressured.

It seemed he owed her an apology.

GUITAR CASE IN HAND, Merry walked into the large, comfortably cluttered family room of her home to find Grant ensconced on the couch, soft drink in hand, watching television with Marsha and Meaghan. She wasn't surprised to see him since she'd just parked her aging blue Caprice beside his gleaming Ferrari.

His expression was just a bit wary when he looked up at her. "Hi. How was your class?"

Very aware of the not-so-subtle interest being given them, Merry set her guitar case on the floor beside a worn armchair. "Fine." She looked away from Grant. "Where's Melinda?"

"She and Savage aren't home yet from the school band concert," Marsha answered. "She's supposed to be home in fifteen minutes."

"Then she will be," Merry said confidently. Savage had been scrupulously careful about curfews so there would be no problems with his continuing to see Melinda.

"Merry, I'd like to talk to you." Grant set his soft drink on the coffee table in front of him and rose.

"All right. Let's go in the kitchen. I'd like a cup of tea."

"Fine."

Not even looking to see if Grant were following, Merry turned and walked to the kitchen, where she went straight to the sink and began to fill a brightly enameled kettle with water. Her head lowered so that her hair fell forward over her face, she busied herself with cup and tea bag. "Can I get you anything, Grant?"

"No, thanks." He fell silent, standing a few feet behind her, but making no effort to draw her attention away from what she was doing.

Finally Merry could stand the silence no longer. "I thought you wanted to talk," she said, tossing her hair back so that she could see him.

"I was waiting for you to look at me," he answered quietly. "I want to apologize for what happened between us on the phone this morning."

Merry dropped her gaze to the cup she was twisting in suddenly cold fingers. "You don't owe me an apology, Grant. I said things to you that I shouldn't have said, and really didn't mean. I'm the one who's sorry."

His hand covered hers, pulling her fingers away from the cup to lace them with his. "No, you were right, love. I was pushing. I know you have other responsibilities, and I promised you that I wouldn't demand too much from you, but I was. It won't happen again."

"No, *you* were right, Grant," Merry argued anxiously. "I was taking out my tension on you. I'm sorry."

Grant chuckled and released her hand to pull her into his arms. "Are we going to stand here all night debating who was at fault? Let's agree that we both overreacted a bit, shall we?"

Her hands sliding up to his shoulders, Merry smiled in relief. "Yes, let's do."

"Kiss and make up?" he asked huskily, his mouth lowering to within an inch of hers.

"Please," she whispered, rising on tiptoe to close the distance.

The kiss was gentle and very sweet, apologies given and accepted on each side. But sweetness soon gave way to hunger, and hunger to passion. Merry wrapped her arms around Grant's neck and opened her mouth to his devastating invasion. His hands went to her waist and then dropped lower to lift her more firmly against him. Merry felt the fine trembling in those big, capable hands. It was happening again, she thought in a haze of wonder. She was being seduced by his obvious need for her. She'd never met a man so open with his emotions and vulnerabilities. And she loved him for it.

Grant pulled his mouth from hers to feather tantalizingly fleeting kisses across her eyelids, her temples, her cheeks and chin. "I love you," he murmured, adoring her face with his lips. "God, how I love you."

The sound she made was part moan, part sob. "Oh, Grant. If you only knew what you do to me."

She was only dimly aware of a shrill whistle coming from somewhere beside them. Her hands cradling Grant's face, she ignored the sound, wanting nothing to intrude on this moment. Grant reached over to twist the knob on the stove, effectively silencing the teakettle. "Do you want your tea?" he asked her softly, his ice-blue eyes blazing into hers.

"No," she answered on a ragged breath. "I want you."

With an inarticulate sound from deep in his throat, he crushed her to him, his mouth coming down on hers with barely restrained ardor. Pressing herself as closely against him as physically possible, Merry gloried in the feel of him, hard and hungry against her accommodating softness. So little separated them. A few layers of fabric. She ached to be even closer, to be joined with him in the most intimate way possible. In Grant's arms there were no problems, no worries. Only blissful, mindless pleasure.

Grant dragged his lips to her ear, his breathing harsh. "It seems like forever since we've been alone," he muttered, one hand tangling in her hair as he continued to press her against him with the other. "I wish—"

"Merry? I'm sorry, but I have to talk to you."

Merry started and turned in Grant's arms to find Melinda standing in the kitchen doorway. The expression on her little sister's face made Merry step away from Grant and hold out her arms. "Melinda, honey, what is it? What's wrong?"

With a heartrending sob Melinda threw herself at Merry. Though she was as tall as her petite sister, Melinda suddenly looked small and very young as she cried into Merry's shoulder. Merry turned a puzzled look at Grant, who hovered close, his face creased in concern, though still slightly flushed with the remnants of passion. "Melinda," Merry said, keeping her voice firm to try to penetrate the teenager's misery. "Tell me what's wrong."

"It's Savage," Melinda answered brokenly. "He...he's leaving Springfield. For good."

"He's leaving? When?"

"As...as soon as he graduates from school next month. He...he said it's best if we don't see each other anymore," she finished on a wail, before breaking into sobs once more.

"Oh, honey, I'm sorry," Merry murmured, remembering how painful teenage heartbreak could be. She looked apologetically at Grant, who nodded his understanding.

"I'll call you tomorrow," he told her quietly. He looked as if he wanted to speak comfortingly to Melinda but didn't know what to say. Touching Merry's shoulder as he passed, he left her to deal with her sister.

His body still taut with frustrated desire, he bypassed the family room and let himself quietly out the front door. Shoving his still-unsteady hand through his rumpled hair, he walked rapidly to his car. "Damn," he muttered, slamming his hand against the smooth red top of the vehicle.

"I know just how you're feeling," a sympathetic voice said from behind him.

Grant whirled to find Savage leaning against the huge oak tree that shaded the front yard of the James home, a glowing cigarette dangling from his fingers. Dressed in baggy military camouflage, the slim young man blended so well into the shadows that the platinum streaks he'd bleached into his brown hair stood out in ghostly contrast. "What are you doing there?"

Savage shrugged and moved a bit so that the gaslight on the other side of the tree cast a golden glow on his sober face. "I just brought Melinda home."

Grant noticed for the first time the vintage black Mustang parked on the side of the street. "Yeah," he growled. "I just left her crying into Merry's shoulder."

Savage drew deeply on the cigarette, then blew the smoke out in a sharp gust. "I know. She's pretty upset."

"She said you're leaving Springfield."

"I am. Soon as I get my diploma in five weeks." Savage reached toward one of the many pockets in his mercenary-issue shirt. "Want a cigarette?"

"No, thanks, I quit a long time ago."

"I just started." Savage gave a dry chuckle and ground the half-smoked cigarette out beneath a booted heel. "Can't say I like it all that much."

"So why'd you start?"

The sideways glance that Savage turned to him was expressive. "Same reason you just almost dented your fancy car," the young man drawled. "Sometimes a man needs something to do with his hands."

Grant was exactly twice Savage's age, but he found himself suddenly feeling as if he had a great deal in common with the boy. No, not a boy, he reminded himself. Savage was almost eighteen. A man. "You're leaving because of Melinda?"

Savage looked down at his scarred boot. "Mostly. There's other reasons, too. Bad home life, bad rep. It's time for me to get away."

"What are you going to do?"

"I signed up for the Navy yesterday. I leave for boot camp in Florida in six weeks."

Grant was surprised and didn't bother to hide it. "The Navy?"

Rather sheepishly, Savage nodded. "Yeah. I was thinking maybe I could get my college degree in the Navy and then go into flight training. It'll take a while, but the recruiter told me I could do it if I put my mind to it."

"Have you by any chance seen the movie *Top Gun*?" Grant smiled companionably as he asked the question.

Savage returned the grin. "Yeah. Great movie, huh?"

Grant nodded. "If I'd seen it when *I* was seventeen, I'd have probably done the same thing you're doing. Guess you know though, you're going to have to lose the pretty hair and the earrings."

"They've served their purpose," Savage replied with another shrug, sounding much too mature for his age.

Grant had little doubt that the young man would accomplish anything he decided he wanted. He hoped he did. "Melinda's going to miss you."

There was no mistaking the pain in the reply. "I'll miss her, too. But I've got to go." He shot a quick glance at Grant. "She's only fourteen. I'd feel like a jerk if I laid a hand on her. Not to mention that her brother would kill me."

"I'd probably kill you myself," Grant agreed equably.

Savage chuckled without much humor and half turned away, then stopped. "Just in case you're wondering, I've got nothing to do with those robberies."

"I know."

Nodding, Savage moved toward his car. "You're all right, Bryant," he tossed over his shoulder.

"You're all right yourself, Taylor."

Savage laughed. "Remember that in a few years when I come back, will you?" He jerked open the door of his Mustang and grinned cockily. "I *will* be back, you know."

Grant watched Savage drive away. He understood the young man's reason for leaving town, even approved of them, but he wished that Savage had waited for a better time to make his announcement. With Matt leaving for Nashville Friday morning and the police investigation involving her business, Merry had enough to worry about without trying to deal with a heartbroken teen-ager.

His heart ached with his concern for her. She had so much to deal with now. He wanted nothing more than to hold her, to make things easier on her, but how? All he knew to do was to be there for her whenever she needed him, yet he was beginning to wonder if his presence weren't adding to her stress, rather than easing it. He wanted her so much, needed her so much, that he couldn't stop himself from making demands on her at times.

He swallowed hard, searching the star-studded sky for answers that just weren't there. Then, with one last wistful look at the house, he climbed into his car and started the engine. It was going to be a long, lonely night.

8

MERRY COULD hardly believe she was having such a good time. She hadn't really expected to enjoy this gathering at her home on Thursday evening—Matt's last night in Springfield—but she couldn't remember laughing so much in a long time. It felt good, she thought, particularly when Grant reached under the huge oak dining table in the James family's dining room and squeezed her thigh with familiar intimacy.

Matt and the twins had added the extra leaf to their grandmother's old table so that it would comfortably accommodate the nine people now seated around it—Merry's brother and sisters and the four guests, Grant, his friend Tim, Boyd and Savage. Merry knew that Savage had originally turned down Melinda's invitation to join them this evening but had been unable to resist his girlfriend's pleas. Merry was glad. Though she realized his departure was going to be painful for Melinda, she was proud of the young man for deciding to make something of himself, and she wanted him to know that he had the support of Melinda's family. Even Matt was making a special effort to be sociable with Savage—now that he knew Savage was leaving town soon.

The evening could have been rather sad, with both Matt's and Savage's departures imminent and Merry's worries about her business increasing with each passing day. Thanks to Grant and Tim, however, sadness was not allowed to set in as the group dived into heaping platters of fried fish and hush puppies. As Melinda commented at one point during the evening, Grant and Tim were better entertainment than a comedy team.

"Better than Martin and Lewis, huh?" Tim asked with a twinkle in his almost-navy-blue eyes.

"Who?" Melinda inquired, her brow puckering.

"How about Crosby and Hope?" Grant suggested. Melinda shook her head, her hands going up to indicate that she had no idea who he was talking about.

Knowing Melinda was feigning ignorance to tease, Merry added her own suggestion. "Abbott and Costello?"

"Yeah. Who's on first!" Tim exclaimed.

"What's on second," Grant responded immediately.

"I don't know," Marsha inserted eagerly.

"Third base!" shouted Merry, Matt, Meaghan, Grant, Tim and Savage while Melinda giggled and Boyd looked around with an expression of rather condescending tolerance.

That young man really is *boring*, Merry thought in annoyance, then turned her attention back to more interesting matters.

"You guys are weird," Melinda proclaimed, shaking her head.

"Do the names Cheech and Chong ring a bell?" Tim inquired dryly.

"Oh, sure." Melinda looked pleased with herself. "They used to be a comedy team." She pretended to be completely perplexed when everyone else laughed.

Tim immediately launched into an improvised pseudo-Hispanic monologue, complete with accent, sending the twins into peals of giggles. Merry smiled as she stabbed her fork into the diminishing pile of coleslaw on her plate. She had greeted Tim earlier with mixed feelings.

Though the handsome, auburn-haired man with the boyish friendly face seemed very nice, she could not help wondering at first if his presence in town would make a difference in the tentative relationship forming between herself and Grant. It was evident that Grant and Tim were close—closer than most brothers, probably. Merry had wondered if Tim would lure Grant away from Springfield to pursue more interesting pleasures than a woman with too many problems and not enough time.

Now that she'd spent almost two hours with him, Merry could tell that Tim was much like Grant. Cheerful, good-humored, but ultimately steady and dependable. Tim Castle was no more suited to comfortable unemployment than Grant. He and Grant had been telling her about their idea for starting a computer consulting firm targeted primarily at small, computer-shy businesses. Realizing that Grant must have been working on the details for the firm for some time, Merry had given him an apologetic look, to which he'd responded with an understanding smile.

Merry had also noted with secret amusement that Tim and Marsha had been surreptitiously checking each other out since Grant had introduced them a couple of hours earlier. There was no way that Marsha could call this one an "overdeveloped, underdeveloped Neanderthal." After dinner Grant volunteered to help Merry clean up while the others retired to the family room to play board games, a favorite pastime for the James family. Sensing that he wanted the time alone with her, no one protested.

Continuing to keep their conversation light and amusing, Grant waited until all the dishes were rinsed and stacked in the dishwasher and the grease splatters from the fish fry wiped up before bringing up a more serious subject. "Will you tell me now what was bothering you earlier?" he asked quietly, cornering her against the counter by placing one hand on either side of her.

Merry looked questioningly up at him, distracted by his proximity. He was so close that his thighs rubbed lightly against hers through their jeans, causing her body temperature to rise abruptly by several degrees. "When?" she asked blankly.

"When I got here tonight, you were pale and your hands were trembling," he elaborated, his gaze drifting downward to the low scooped neckline of her black-and-turquoise figured sweater. "What happened?"

"There was another robbery last night," she admitted. "It happened during the party. One of the guests who lives in Brentwood was only at the party for about two and a half hours, and he was home by ten o'clock, but his house had already been hit. Sheriff Roland and Detective Litchfield were back at the office today, and this time they stayed awhile. They're questioning all my employees, particularly Kirk and Louis, who didn't work last night. They're still asking a lot of questions about Savage, but at least they've decided that you're not a suspect. No thanks to you. You almost had them convinced the other day that you were an unemployed drifter who moved in on me to get at my clients."

"What made them change their minds?"

"They investigated you," she answered sardonically. "They probably know as much about you as your sister, right down to how much you paid for your car and how much is left in your bank account in Colorado."

Grant winced. "I suppose I should be pleased that they're so thorough. Maybe that will protect you and your employees from being unjustly carted off to jail."

Merry couldn't smile. She turned her face and bit her lower lip as her earlier concerns returned in a depressing rush.

"That's not all, is it?" Grant asked perceptively.

She shook her head. "I had a couple of calls today. People are beginning to talk about MerryMakers' connection to the robberies. One woman who had not yet paid a deposit canceled the party we'd been discussing, saying that she didn't want to take the risk of any of her friends being robbed."

"Oh, honey, I'm sorry." Grant pulled her into his arms. "No wonder you're so tense."

"All it takes is something like this to ruin a small business." She leaned her head against his shoulder and closed her eyes, drawing strength from his embrace. "We've just really started making a profit, and now this could destroy us. Marsha and I have worked so hard to build our business, Grant."

"You're not going to lose your business, Merry," Grant promised, hoping he wasn't being overly optimistic. "Once it's been proved that neither your company nor anyone involved with it is connected—"

"But, Grant." Merry lifted her head from his shoulder to look up at him with troubled eyes. "Someone from my company could well be involved! I don't want to believe it, but someone is finding out who's attending these parties and using that information to rob their homes. MerryMakers is the only thing that any of these crimes have in common!"

He exhaled and dropped his head to rest his forehead against hers. "I know. I wish there was something I could do."

"I've started locking up guest lists, not even releasing them to the photographer in advance. But I'm still worried. Leida's party is Saturday afternoon and she's invited a lot of people. What if something happens then? I'd feel terrible if one of your sister's friends was victimized because of my company."

"Merry, Leida's party is during the middle of the afternoon. Besides, you know she'd never blame you if anything did happen."

Merry nodded and slipped her arms around his waist. "Let's just hope nothing does."

Grant held her tightly for a time, then lowered his head to kiss her. "It feels good to have you in my arms again."

"It feels good to be here," she answered with a wistful smile.

"Want to go to your bedroom?"

She laughed softly, pushing her problems out of her mind. "I don't allow the twins to entertain boys in their bedroom. They'd never let me get away with it."

Rocking her a little in the circle of his arms, he smiled with boyish charm. "Want to go to your office?"

"Mmm. I wish we could." She rose on tiptoe to plant a kiss on his uptilted mouth. "Guess we'd better resign ourselves to board games with the family.

"That's not much of a substitute," Grant complained, sliding his hand down her spine to settle warmly at her hip.

"It's the best I can offer tonight."

He kissed her, then murmured against her mouth, "I'll take what I can get. I love you, Merry."

"Oh, Grant, I—"

"I thought it was taking an awfully long time to do the dishes," Matt said in amusement from the doorway.

Grant exhaled forcefully and spoke to Merry. "Have you noticed that every time I kiss you lately, someone interrupts us?"

She smiled, pulling reluctantly out of his arms. "I've noticed. What do you want, Matthew?"

"I just came in for soft drinks for everyone. And to find out whether this man is molesting my sister." Closest to Merry in both age and appearance, Matt smiled with obvious approval at the couple in front of him.

"Your sister couldn't get molested in this house if she tried," Merry grumbled teasingly. She winked at Grant. "And I *have* tried."

Laughing, Matt enlisted Merry and Grant's help in serving soft drinks to the thirsty crowd in the family room, who were involved in a complicated board game for which they'd divided into teams.

Tim looked up as Merry and Grant entered the room. "Hey, Grant, Matt said he'd give us directions to the lake where he caught all those crappie we had for dinner. What do you say to a fishing trip tomorrow morning?"

"Sounds good."

"Grant, I've been trying to remember ever since you and Tim brought up that old Abbott and Costello routine—who's in left field?" Marsha asked.

"No, Marsha, Who's on first," Tim spoke up quickly from his seat next to her, turning one of his bright smiles toward her. "Why's left field."

"Why's left field what?" Melinda demanded.

"What's on second," Grant spoke up, dropping onto the couch and tugging Merry down beside him.

"I don't care," Melinda moaned dramatically.

"Short stop!" came a shout from several of the others.

Smiling, Merry settled comfortably into the curve of Grant's arm and wished that she could hold on to the warmth and humor present in the room with her now to give her strength against whatever might wait for her tomorrow.

"WELL, WHAT DO YOU THINK of Merry?"

"I think you're out of your mind if you don't marry that woman immediately," Tim pronounced firmly. "She's great. Her whole family's great."

Grant smiled as he smoothly cast his hook into the clear blue water, then settled back against the seat of the rented fishing boat to wait for a strike. "I knew you'd like them."

"So how come you're just now asking my opinion?" Tim inquired lazily, tugging his baseball-style cap low over his forehead to block the morning sun.

Grant shrugged. "I had to work up my nerve," he confessed. "I never introduced you to a woman I intend to marry before."

"I can see where that might make you a bit nervous," Tim teased.

"How'd you like Merry's beautiful blond sisters?"

Shaking his head in disgust at the empty hook he'd just reeled in, Tim reached for another cricket out of the wire-sided bait box. "You might have told me that two of those beautiful blond sisters were still in junior high."

"That leaves one who's available."

"Marsha? Yeah, she's okay."

"Just okay?"

"A little young. She's twelve years younger than I am, you know."

Grant shrugged. "I've always thought you were immature for your age," he teased.

Tim shot a reproachful look at his friend. "Hey, buddy, just because you're starting to think mortgages and diapers doesn't mean you have to push me in that direction."

Grant chuckled and gave a tug on his graphite rod as a hungry crappie took his bait. "Sorry. I hear it's a side effect of being in love to try to match up all your friends."

"This is truly disgusting," Tim muttered, shaking his head as he morosely watched Grant pull in a good-sized crappie. "You've turned completely sappy on me. You never talked like this when you were going out with Dolores."

Grant shook his head vehemently. "No comparison. Now that I've met Merry, I can't remember what I saw in Dolores in the first place."

"Do the numbers 36-25-36 refresh your memory?"

Grant made a production of storing his catch in the live-well between them, ignoring Tim's wry question.

After a few minutes of companionable silence Tim spoke again a bit sheepishly. "Actually, I thought Marsha was very nice. I asked her for dinner tomorrow night, after Leida's party. But don't start gloating," he added quickly. "I like her, but that's all for now, okay?"

"Not everyone is perceptive enough to know what he wants with just one look," Grant uttered in a superior tone that earned him an empty beer can tossed at his head. He laughed and caught the missile before it fell into the lake, dropping it to lie with an empty can at his feet. And then his mood grew suddenly pensive. "I wish the cops would wrap up this robbery thing. It's really worrying Merry."

"I can imagine. Something like this could be disastrous for her company. You've met all her employees?"

"All but Anne. They seem okay, and Merry swears each one is honest."

"You told me on the phone the other day that you had a couple of ideas. Want to share?"

"I have one suspect," Grant admitted. "But not a shred of evidence."

"So tell me about it. Between the two of us, maybe we can come up with something."

"Since when are you into crime-solving?"

Tim grinned. "Well, we could always be a private-eye team if this other idea of yours doesn't pan out. I always rather fancied being a gumshoe."

"You've been reading old murder mysteries again, haven't you?" Grant demanded.

"Never mind that. Tell me your suspect and let's get busy solving your lady's case. I've never been a best man before, and I happen to look great in a tux."

Grant turned his head to busy himself with his fishing rod, hoping that Tim had missed the longing expression that he knew full well had just crossed his face. Unlike Tim, Grant wasn't so sure that a wedding would automatically follow the solution of the robberies that were threatening Merry's business. Despite his confidence that they belonged together, he had yet to convince her. He was fully aware that she had not even told him that she loved him.

THEIR DARK HEADS CLOSE together, Merry and Matt sat side by side on the small vinyl couch in her office. "I'm really going to miss you, Matt."

Matt draped an arm around his eldest sister's shoulders and pulled her into a rough hug. "I'll miss you, too, Merry. I hate leaving you today with all this worry about the robberies."

"I know. But you have no choice. This job is a wonderful opportunity for you."

"It really is." Matt's leaf-green eyes, so like his older sister's, glowed with excitement. "I've always wanted to manage a big, beautiful hotel like the Amber Rose. I know I'll only be assistant manager now, but there's a good chance that I'll be promoted again in a few years."

"I'm sure you will." Merry smiled proudly at the younger brother who had helped her through so many hard times. Matt had been forced to mature fast when their parents had died, as had Merry and Marsha, and he had grown into a dependable, warmhearted, responsible man. A bit arrogant at times, Merry added to herself in mild amusement, thinking of the rather high-handed way he'd tried to help her raise the twins. But he always meant well. "I love you, Matt."

"I love you, too," he responded gruffly. "You'll call me if you need me? For anything, even just to talk."

"I'll call you."

"And if you need to send the twins to me for any reason, do so. I hope this investigation is over soon, but if it's still going on when school's out in a few weeks, or if you just want a vacation, put them on a flight to Nashville and I'll ride herd for a couple of weeks."

"Making the supreme sacrifice, huh?" Merry laughed lovingly at him. "What about your job?"

"I'll chain them to a television while I'm working," he replied ruefully. "Seriously, though, I think they'd love Nashville. It's a beautiful city. I want you all to come visit me there soon."

"We will. And don't forget that you can come home to Springfield occasionally, will you?"

"You bet. I won't be able to stay away from my family for very long."

Merry clung tightly to his hand as she looked at him for a long, silent moment, knowing he would have to leave soon. He was tanned and slim and terribly attractive. Merry had often teased him about being the truly beautiful one in the family, to his disgust. His air of casual self-confidence lent him a maturity beyond his twenty-five years.

"Want to talk about that big guy you met a little over a week ago who now seems to consider himself a member of the family?" Matt asked with a smile, using the teasing comment to lighten her suddenly sad mood.

"Not particularly," Merry replied with a grimace.

"Well, I do. He's okay, Merry. I'm glad he's around."

"I can't tell you how relieved that makes me," she drawled sarcastically. "It's nice to know that Grant has won over the entire family."

Matt's left eyebrow quirked upward in an expression she recognized. "Problem?"

She shook her head. "No, not really. It's just that sometimes lately I've had the impression that my life is moving ahead of me. Kind of out of control, you know?"

"I know how you would hate feeling out of control of anything," he admitted. "You've been in charge for too long."

Merry frowned worriedly, pondering his words. "Have I turned into a managing type of woman, Matt? I don't want being responsible for the kids and the business to turn me into a demi-dictator."

He chuckled. "I'm not sure what that means, but you're not one, whatever it is. It's just that you have an overdeveloped sense of responsibility."

"And you don't," she countered.

He shrugged. "Okay, I do. Comes from being the eldest son and eldest daughter, eh?"

"I suppose so." But she was still a bit concerned about his suggestion that she had to always be in control. Did Grant see her that way? she wondered.

"I have to go, Merry. It's a long drive to Nashville."

"You'll let me know you're there safely?"

"Yeah. I'll call you when I get there."

"Okay." Fighting an unwelcome rush of tears, Merry stood and threw her arms around her brother's neck, hugging him fiercely before stepping back. "Be careful."

"I will." His own eyes suspiciously bright, Matt turned away and walked into the reception area, where he hugged and kissed Marsha. He'd said his farewells to the twins that morning before they'd left for school.

After Matt had gone, Merry and Marsha looked at each other, sniffled, then smiled shakily.

"Will it be like this when the twins go away to college?" Marsha inquired with a husky catch in her voice.

"Probably," Merry answered with a weak smile. "Our children seem to be growing up, don't they?"

Marsha nodded, then smiled, her naturally mischievous sense of humor coming out. "So why don't you get busy making some more? I wouldn't mind spoiling a couple of nieces and nephews now that the twins are getting too big to baby."

Merry flushed. "Why don't *you* provide some more?" she retorted.

Marsha laughed. "I'm not the one with a perfectly nice man bound and determined to pursue me."

"Given a little encouragement, there's one who might give it a shot."

This time it was Marsha's turn to flush. "Tim? I barely know him, Merry."

"Yeah. That's what I was saying last week about Grant," Merry grumbled. "But did anybody listen? *No-o-o-o!*"

Grant and Tim dropped into the office after lunch, freshly showered, noses a bit reddened from the water-reflected sun they'd exposed themselves to that morning. Smiling a welcome, Merry thought again that the bond between the two men was a strong one. She was glad that Grant had such a good friend, and that both of them seemed eager to settle down in Springfield.

"Catch any fish?" she inquired.

"You bet," Tim answered promptly.

"I caught most of them," Grant bragged boyishly, earning himself an exaggerated scowl from his friend. Laughing, Grant changed the subject. "We're here to offer a suggestion, Merry."

"Uh-oh." She looked at them suspiciously. "What kind of suggestion?"

"We want you to call in the whole crew for Leida's party tomorrow. Linda, Kirk, Anne and Louis. Tell them you need them all."

"Okay, but why?"

"We'll explain later," he answered vaguely. "Also, I want you to have your entire family there, as well as Boyd and Savage."

"You want Boyd and Savage to come to your sister's party?" Marsha repeated, looking puzzled as she came in on the conversation. "Why?"

"It won't look so strange," Tim explained. "The party's in Grant's honor, right? It's only natural for Leida to invite the family he's become such good friends with."

"We could always tell everyone we have an important announcement to make," Grant suggested smoothly, slipping an arm around Merry's waist.

She shot him a warning look. "I'll get everyone there," she informed him reprovingly.

"What are you two up to, anyway?" Marsha demanded.

Tim cocked his head, glancing at Grant. "Should we tell all, Holmes?"

"Not just yet, Watson. Either one of them could be the crook," Grant returned with a poorly concealed grin.

"This one does look a bit suspicious," Tim agreed, leaning close to Marsha and staring into her laughing gray eyes. "Maybe I should frisk her."

"Keep your hands off my sister," Merry growled with mock ferocity.

"Good idea," Grant proclaimed immediately. "I'll search this one. Back in five minutes." He hustled an unresisting Merry into her office and closed the door on Marsha and Tim's laughter. "Come here, you."

"I love it when you sweet-talk me," Merry murmured, walking into his outstretched arms.

He kissed her lingeringly, then lifted his head with a private, intimate smile. "Hi."

She shivered at the evocatively husky tone of the one word. "Hi," she whispered in return.

He kissed her again. "You're beautiful today. I like that red dress. But then, you're always beautiful."

"Whatever you want, the answer is yes," she murmured with a ripple of humor, her hands locking behind his neck.

He chuckled. "Think I'm only complimenting you because I want something?"

"Aren't you?"

"*Now* who's fishing?" he teased, hugging her.

"Grant, why do you want me to have everyone at the party tomorrow?"

"Just a hunch," he answered unsatisfactorily, then immediately changed the subject. "Are you free for a couple of hours tonight?"

"I have a few things to get ready for Leida's party, but I could take a couple of hours. Why?"

"I've made an appointment with a Realtor to see that house I like in Cinnamon Square. Will you go with me?"

She hesitated, then moistened her lips. "What time?" she asked, trying to hide her sudden attack of nerves.

"Six o'clock?"

"Okay. Want to pick me up here?"

He hugged her again. "Thanks, Merry. I really want you to see it with me. And be honest, okay? If you don't like it, say so."

Merry worked up the courage to be blunt. "Grant, are you buying this house with the intention of living in it with me?"

"Of course I am," he answered, equally forthright. "I've told you that I love you. I want to marry you. You had to know that I was serious."

She swallowed hard. "You haven't even asked me to marry you."

He grinned broadly, almost masking the vulnerability in his eyes. "I told you, I avoid a lot of rejection that way."

She took a deep breath and stepped reluctantly out of his arms. "Don't rush me, Grant. Please."

"I'm trying very hard not to rush you. But I can't stop hoping or making plans." The determined look in his cool blue eyes warned her that he was willing to give her only as much time as he thought she needed.

"I'll look at the house with you, Grant, but I don't want you to take that as a sign that I consider the future settled, do you understand? As long as this robbery thing is threatening my business, I couldn't possibly think about anything else so monumental." She was trying hard to sound firm.

Grant released a sharp breath and nodded. "I'll pick you up here at six." Merry nodded, chewing her lower lip as she accompanied Grant back into the reception area. With a twinge of regret she realized that some of the high spirits he'd entered with earlier had diminished, and that she was at fault. But, dammit, why was he so determined to rush her, despite his claims to the contrary? she thought irritably.

Tim was perched on one corner of Marsha's desk, chatting with her as he waited for Grant. His dark blue eyes went quickly from Grant's face to Merry's, but he said only, "Are you ready to go?"

Grant nodded. "Yeah. They need to get back to work, and we've got some business prospects to check out. See you at six, Merry. Bye Marsha."

"Don't tell me the two of you quarreled again," Marsha wailed when Grant and Tim were gone.

Merry shook her head dispiritedly. "No, we didn't quarrel. We—Oh, hell, I don't know what we did."

The telephone buzzed and Merry welcomed the distraction. "I'll get that," she said, whirling on one heel to hurry to her desk.

9

THERE WAS NO DOUBT about it. The house was beautiful. Only two years old, it was a spacious two-story
contemporary of stone and glass. Downstairs contained
a formal living room, a huge den, a dream of a kitchen,
dining room, guest bath and an enormous master bedroom with a sinfully appointed private bath. A cozy
nook near the master bedroom could serve as a nursery
or a study. Three more bedrooms and two baths were
upstairs, along with a paneled game room complete with
wet bar. "It's fantastic," Merry murmured in awe. "It's
also huge."

"I particularly like the deck in back and the big fenced-
in backyard," Grant told her enthusiastically. "Great
family home, isn't it?"

"It's so big," Merry said again, staring around her.

"It's made for a big family." The realtor had remained
downstairs, leaving Grant and Merry to look around in
privacy, and Grant took advantage of the opportunity
to put his arms around her. "There are plenty of bedrooms for the twins. Not to mention that nursery."

"No, let's not mention the nursery," Merry muttered,
stepping nervously out of his arms. "What about Marsha?"

He shrugged one shoulder. "Marsha would be welcome in our home at any time, of course, and there's still
an extra bedroom, but don't you think she's probably

ready to have her own place? She's twenty-two, after all. She may even prefer to stay in the house where she is."

"I like our house, too," Merry argued, knowing it wasn't the time for such a discussion but somehow unable to stop herself. "Why couldn't we live there—if we decided to get married, of course," she added hastily.

"Merry, your parents' home is a good size, but it's an older house with older-house problems, and it's not as big as this one. Besides, I wouldn't be comfortable moving into a house that belongs to you and your brother and sisters. I want to invest in my own place."

"Oh, this house would belong to you, would it?"

Grant's eyes narrowed. "If you and I were married, this house would belong to both of us. Equally. You know that."

"I have a house."

"Fine. You can keep it, or sell it and split the money into trust funds or education money, or whatever you like. I'd no more tell you what to do with your personal property than I'd tell you how to run your business."

"The twins have never lived in another house. Maybe they wouldn't want to move." Merry crossed her arms over her chest and glared at him, not sure herself where her sudden hostility was coming from.

"Dammit, Merry, you're testing me again! How do you want me to respond this time?" Grant exploded, shoving his hands deep into the pockets of his dark slacks as if afraid of what he might do with them if he left them free.

Her eyes opened wide. "What do you mean, testing you?"

He looked as if he regretted the words. "Never mind. Forget it."

"No," she insisted. "I want to know. How am I testing you?"

"All right, I'll tell you. You've been testing me since the day we met," he informed her in a low, angry voice. "The minute you realized that I was attracted to you, that I was starting to care for you, you decided that I didn't know what I was getting myself into, that I wouldn't want to take on your responsibilities, didn't you? Each new problem that has cropped up since then has been a new test, a new reason for you to wonder if I'll have had enough. *I am not Justin, Merry!*"

She felt herself pale, clenching her hands behind her back. "I never said you were."

"No, but you sure don't trust me to know my own mind, do you?" he accused her furiously.

"No, I don't!" she flared. "How could I? Dammit, Grant, look at this from my viewpoint. You've known me for nine days! *Nine days, Grant!* And you've already declared that you love me, announced that you're going to marry me and found a house for us to live in. What am I supposed to think?"

"You're supposed to think that I have the sense to know a good thing when I find it," he answered bitterly. "You're supposed to understand that I knew I was in love with you by the time I'd taken two letters from you that first afternoon. You're supposed to realize that I've been looking for you all my life and that I've been so happy about finding you that I couldn't make myself move slowly and cautiously with you."

"Even—" She had to stop to clear her throat of an enormous lump. "Even if I could believe that everything was that simple for you, what makes you think that I feel the same way?"

He met her eyes without blinking. "Because you made love with me exactly two days after we met. Don't try to tell me you would have given yourself to me that afternoon unless you'd been pretty damned sure about your feelings for me. I know you, Merry James. You don't sleep around, and you don't give in to mere physical attraction. You made love with me because you were in love with me, didn't you? *Didn't you?*" he roared when she could not immediately answer.

"Uh, excuse me," a hesitant voice said from the doorway of the game room. "Is there a problem with you folks?"

Merry turned her stricken gaze to the jittery little man in the bright gold coat who was watching them with an expression of concern. For the life of her, she couldn't think of anything to say.

Grant jerked his hands out of his pockets and turned his back on Merry, facing the real-estate agent. "No, Mr. Calhoun, there's no problem. Thank you for letting us look around. We'll let you know our decision."

"Of course." The balding fellow glanced furtively at Merry's tight face before ushering them out of the house.

The atmosphere in Grant's car was strained, the silence between its occupants oppressive. Merry could feel the beginnings of another headache just making itself felt. She kept her face turned to the side window, though every nerve in her body was trained on Grant.

"We have to finish this, you know," he said at length. "And we can't do it at your house in front of an audience. Should we go to the office?"

She shook her head. "We wouldn't be able to talk there. Marsha and Kirk are there, getting things ready for Leida's party tomorrow. I should be helping them."

He exhaled gustily. "Damn."

She blinked against a rush of hot tears, forcing them back. "It's always like this with me, Grant. There's always something that has to be done. Maybe I can learn to manage my hours more efficiently, and I'm certainly willing to try, but it's too soon to consider all our problems solved. I can't make a commitment to you until I'm sure it will work between us. Can't you understand that?"

He pulled into her driveway and shoved the gearshift into Park. "I understand that you still don't trust me," he replied bleakly. "You think I'll grow tired of your responsibilities, that I'll change my mind about wanting to marry you. You say you know I'm different from Justin, but you don't really believe it, do you?"

She turned to him beseechingly, her hands gripped painfully in her lap. "Grant, all I'm asking is that you don't push me. Why can't you accept the fact that nine days isn't long enough for me to abandon all caution and leap into an engagement with you?"

"So what do you want from me, Merry?" He turned his head until his gaze was boring into hers, demanding an answer. "Do you want to date? Go steady, like the twins? Sneak around to make love? Is that what you want?"

She lifted one hand to her temple, then dropped it hastily into her lap when she realized that it was shaking. "You make it sound so sordid," she protested. "As if there was something wrong with dating."

He shook his head. "It's not that. If I thought you were only concerned about time, I wouldn't care. Much. But I think it's more than that."

"I don't—"

He interrupted her. "Let me put it another way, Merry. Do you want to stop seeing me? Is that it? Should I go back to Colorado and let you go back to the way your life was before I crashed into it?"

His voice was so devoid of emotion that Merry would have thought he couldn't have cared less about her answer had she not been looking straight into his eyes. As it was, she saw his pain and his vulnerability and her heart twisted. "No," she whispered desolately. "I don't want you to leave."

"I love you, Merry. I wish that I were the type to wait patiently around until you decide you're ready for what I want to give you, but I don't know if I can. Already I'm going nuts wanting to be with you, share your life with you. Wanting to help you with all your problems, try to ease some of the burden on you. Sleeping alone when I want so desperately to have you in my arms. If I'd been the type to wait patiently for life to give me what I want, I'd never have been a success in business. And all my instincts tell me that if I stop pressuring you, if I allow you to take your own time, you'll manage to drive us apart with your fears and insecurities. I'm not going to let you do that."

She felt the faintest ripple of anger. "I won't be forced into something I'm not ready for, Grant. I'm quite capable of making my own decisions. I've been doing so for a long time."

"Yes, you have," he agreed coolly. "And in the process you've lost the ability to trust the judgment of others. You've convinced yourself that your business and your family would fall apart if you gave any less of yourself to either, even though Marsha is a smart woman fully capable of running MerryMakers if necessary and your sisters are growing into capable, responsible young people."

"You really believe I'm that arrogant?" she asked tightly, stung by his criticism.

His eyes softened. "Not arrogant, Merry. I believe your attitude has evolved from necessity, that you've responded to the strain of having too much responsibility at too young an age. The things you've accomplished in the past five years are amazing. You've raised a terrific family and you've started a successful business. But now you have to start letting go, taking care of your own needs for a change."

"And you think I need you?" she whispered.

"I'm praying you do," he answered rawly, "because God only knows how much I need you."

Her head was throbbing. Merry reached up to rub her temples in a gesture that had become all too common lately. "Please, Grant. Please give me a little time. I can't deal with this tonight."

He pulled her gently into his arms. "I know I'm pushing you, Merry. As I said, it's one of my worst faults—impatience. The more you hold back, the more I tend to forge ahead. I guess we both need to make some adjustments. And maybe you're right. Maybe it will take time."

She nodded into his shoulder, unable to speak for the moment.

"I love you, Merry James. I'm not going to let you go now that I've found you. If I have to learn to be patient, then I'll learn."

"You're so sure of yourself," she murmured, clinging to his strength. "So positive that you know what you want after such a short time."

"I knew after spending less than an hour with you," he told her with a short, husky laugh. "I think I knew the moment I looked into your eyes. Maybe it was only nine days ago that we actually met, but I've been waiting for you for thirty-four years. When I saw you, I knew."

He stopped and forced a smile. "I guess it's in my blood. My dad did the same thing with my mother."

"Did he?" Merry tilted her head, intrigued by this bit of Grant's history.

"Yeah. He was with the RAF in '42 when he met my mother. She was a secretary in London."

"Your parents were British?" Merry asked in surprise, amazed at how much she still didn't know about this man who'd become so very important to her.

"Mom was. Like many idealistic young Americans, Dad went to Canada to sign up with the RAF in '41, before Pearl Harbor. He met my mom only two weeks before he was due to be shipped out of London. Took him about five minutes to decide he wanted to marry her, and he did so a week later. Leida was born nine months after their wedding night. Mom told me years later that she never quite knew what hit her."

"I know how she felt. It's like being carried in the path of a tornado," she told him, the left corner of her mouth dipping in her off-centered smile. "You swept into my life and turned everything upside down. I've responded to you harder and faster than anyone before you, and I'm so afraid that I'll never be content with my life again if you suddenly decide to leave."

Touched by her candid words, Grant cupped her face in his large, gentle palms and looked down at her so tenderly that it brought tears to her eyes. "Trust me, Merry," he said simply.

"I can't," she whispered through her tears. "Not yet."

"Then I'll keep working on you until you do," he promised. He lowered his head slowly, his lips just covering hers. He was in no hurry to deepen the kiss, but savored the moist softness of her lips for a long time, until she ached for more. She opened to him invitingly. Grant moaned softly and slanted his head to a new angle, finally allowing himself access to the sweet depths of her mouth.

Her tongue eagerly joined him in a dance of passion and need. The love she couldn't quite bring herself to reveal to him verbally declared itself in her kiss. Grant would have had to be totally insensitive to her not to feel it. Yet he knew already that she loved him. How could he not know after they'd made love with such devastating honesty? If only he could convince her to trust in his love for her.

Breaking the kiss before it could flame completely out of control, he buried his face in her silky hair and held her as if he'd never let her go. But eventually he had to.

MERRY MUTTERED a frustrated expletive and threw off the sheet that had covered her restless body during the past hour while she'd tried and failed to sleep. Another not-for-mixed company word escaped her when she banged her shin solidly on one corner of her nightstand as she climbed out of bed. All right, she thought resentfully. So her room *was* small. All the bedrooms in the house she'd lived in for so long were small. The twins barely had space in their shared room for their single beds and all the clutter they seemed to collect. She thought of the house she'd looked at with Grant earlier. There was plenty of room there. Each twin could have her own bedroom....

No! She would not think of that now. Thinking of Grant, of his plans for her future, of her own insecurities about that future had kept her tossing and turning in her bed on a night when she should be resting up for the big party Leida was giving the next afternoon.

She needed a glass of milk, maybe a handful of cookies, she decided abruptly. Not bothering to cover her mid thigh-length cotton nightshirt with a robe, she left her room and walked quietly through the dark, silent house to the kitchen. The light from the refrigerator made her blink as she pulled out the milk container. Leaving the refrigerator door open for light, she lifted the lid on a ceramic elephant cookie jar and dug out a couple of slightly overbrowned chocolate chip cookies the twins had made that afternoon. Then she shut the refrigerator door and sat down in the dark at the table to eat her snack.

"I love you."

Merry choked on a bite of cookie. Grant's voice had whispered through her head as clearly as if he'd been sitting beside her at the tiny kitchen table. She shivered as with a sudden chill and tossed the second half of the cookie into a wastebasket.

His voice had been so raw, his emotions so apparent. Was it possible that he could love her that much?

She hid her face in her hands, elbows propped on the table. It was scary, she thought, to have someone feel like that about her. No one ever had before. Certainly not Justin, who had treated her like a favorite possession. Justin had turned away from her reluctantly, but he *had* turned away. He hadn't had any doubts about whether he'd be able to live without her.

"God only knows how much I need you."

"Oh, Grant," she moaned aloud. She could acknowledge to herself now that she'd picked a fight with him in the house he'd shown her because she'd felt almost as if she were being given a glimpse of a tantalizing, coveted future that could well be taken away from her once she admitted how very much she wanted it.

She knew how desperately she had grown to love Grant, but not until today had she truly believed he felt the same way about her. But what if his feelings didn't last? What if he found that he couldn't deal with her life? Or what if he lost interest in her once he and Tim were involved in their own new business? He was a self-admitted workaholic. How could they have any kind of a relationship if both of them were totally involved in their careers?

"What are you worrying about now?"

Merry jerked her head around to find a shadowy figure standing in the doorway of the kitchen, watching her. "Meaghan? What are you doing up?"

"Geez, Merry," the teenager complained, snapping on the overhead light and wincing at its brightness. "Even Grant can tell us apart!"

"Oh, sorry, Melinda. You looked like Meaghan in the dark."

"I look like Meaghan in the light," Melinda pointed out prosaically, "but you can usually tell us apart. Could be you had something else on your mind?"

"Could be," Merry agreed. She watched her younger sister fill a glass with milk. "What are you doing up? Couldn't you sleep?"

"I heard you get up a little while ago and I thought I'd keep you company for a few minutes. What's bugging you? The robberies? The business? You and Grant?"

"All of the above." Merry sighed and pushed her tousled hair back from her face.

"You worry too much, sis. But I think I've told you that before."

Merry propped her chin on the heel of her hand and watched Melinda dip a cookie into her milk. "*Do* I worry too much, Melinda?"

"Yep," the girl answered unhesitatingly. "If you don't have anything legit to worry about, you make something up."

Merry frowned. "Not that bad, surely!"

"What can I say?" Melinda chewed, swallowed and took a swig of milk, leaving a damp mustache on her downy upper lip. "You're compulsive. Eldest child syndrome."

"Thank you, Dr. James." Merry's tone was dry as she slowly rolled her milk glass between her hands.

Melinda shrugged. "I've been reading up on it. I think I'll be a psychologist. I get into studying what makes people tick."

"That's an admirable career goal. I didn't realize you were interested in psychology."

"Yeah. Savage got me started on it. He loves to read books on psychology. You should hear him talk about Adler and Jung and Skinner—all those guys."

Merry blinked, knowing that she must be wearing a blank expression. "I thought Savage had decided to be a pilot."

"Oh, he has. Psychology is just one of the things he's interested in. He likes philosophy, too. I can't even pronounce the names of the philosophers he reads."

Not for the first time since she'd known the young man, Merry reflected that there was a great deal hidden behind the outrageous facade Savage affected so deliberately. Her thoughts drifted back to Melinda's accusation. "You know, Matt told me earlier that I'm in danger of becoming a managing woman, and Grant told me I can't trust anyone's judgment except my own. Now you say I worry too much. All these compliments just might go to my head."

"Don't let any of us bother you, Merry. You're the greatest. You've got that super business and you're really good at it. You're raising us and doing a wonderful job. You hardly ever let yourself get in a bad mood, or if you do, you try not to show it. You're gorgeous and fun and smart, and I'd give anything to be just like you."

Merry fought back tears, thinking that they had been threatening on and off all day. "Why, thank you, Melinda. That means a lot to me."

"It's the truth. Sure, you worry a lot, but then, you have a lot of responsibility. I wish there was something I could do to help out more."

"You help me a lot, honey. You all do, just by giving me no reason to worry about you more than necessary. I'm very proud of my younger sisters and brother."

Melinda flushed, typically uncomfortable with such fulsome praise. She munched on a second cookie to avoid having to answer.

"My life hasn't been so bad, Melinda." Merry wanted to make that quite clear. "I've never done anything I didn't really want to do in the first place. My only regret is that Mom and Dad couldn't have been with us longer. But as for being responsible for you and Meaghan...well, I consider myself very fortunate to have you."

Melinda drained her glass, wiped her mouth with the back of her hand and shoved herself out of her chair. "This is too mushy for me," she teased, straightening the top of her shorty pajamas as she rinsed out her glass. "I'm going back to bed."

"Thanks for keeping me company... and for the pat on the back."

Melinda returned Merry's smile with a high-voltage one of her own. "Anytime, kid. I owe you a few. See you in the morning."

She really had led a good life so far, Merry reflected as she rinsed her own glass. Marred only by the tragic death of her parents, it had been a happy and fulfilling life, rich with love and personally satisfying. Though Justin's defection had hurt at the time, she could only be glad now that she had not married him. She wondered absently if they actually would have been married, even if her parents had not died.

An uncomfortable thought struck her as she climbed back into her bed. Was it possible that she really *was* judging Grant based on Justin's defection, as he'd accused her of doing? That would be completely unfair of her. And yet Justin had demanded too much from her and then abandoned her when she couldn't give him what he asked. What if Grant . . . ?

She groaned and pulled the covers up to her chin. No, she wouldn't think about that anymore tonight. She'd think of something else.

If only the police investigation would be concluded before it destroyed the business she loved so much.

No, she thought, shaking her head on the pillows. She wouldn't think of that, either. She would only think of the good things. Like the way Grant looked when he told her he loved her. The way his mouth felt against hers. The way he made her feel that she was the most desirable, most sensuous woman in the world when he made love to her. And the tantalizing prospect of being married to him, living in that beautiful house, not having to slip around to make love, waking up every morning in his arms.

Her lips curving into a faint smile, she snuggled into her pillow and finally drifted off to sleep.

LEIDA'S PARTY BEGAN at two on Saturday afternoon. The day was beautiful—sunny and notably warm even for Missouri in the spring. Merry breathed a sigh of relief as the weather—the only part of the party she hadn't retained full control over—cooperated with the Hawaiian luau theme Leida had chosen. Dressed in a brilliantly patterned tropical dress, Merry cast a quick glance around Leida's back lawn, where colorfully dressed, paper-lei-bedecked guests mingled around the pool, which was filled with floating flower wreaths. Buffet tables laden with Hawaiian-style snacks—pork tidbits and pineapple chunks grilled on skewers, tropical fruits— were decorated with centerpieces constructed of pineapples, banana leaves and flowers. Fruit drinks and some lightly spiked tropical drinks were being served in tumblers decorated with little parasols. Soon the entertainment would begin—a band to play authentic Hawaiian music and Hawaiian dancers to perform and then lead the guests in lighthearted hula lessons.

Everything was going beautifully. Merry should have been deeply pleased. But she felt lousy.

Though she'd fallen asleep in a reasonably happy frame of mind, she had awakened with a pounding headache and her throat feeling as if it had been filled with sand. It hadn't helped that, barely half an hour after she'd forced herself out of bed, she'd had another call from a frequent MerryMakers' client who had heard the rumors about Merry's company being investigated for involvement with the recent rash of robberies. The client had demanded to know if Merry suspected any of her employees of being involved, insinuating that Merry would protect even a guilty employee to save her business's reputation.

Merry had managed to conclude the call without losing her temper, but it hadn't been easy. And then she had thrown herself into the final preparations for Leida's party, determined that it would be the best party MerryMakers had ever organized.

"It's a great party, love."

Merry turned her head to smile rather wanly at Grant. He looked casual and appealing in the purple-and-yellow aloha shirt that Leida had purchased and insisted he wear. Merry had laughed earlier when he'd told her that though he'd agreed to wear the shirt, he had categorically refused to wear the knee-length shorts that matched it. "Are you having a nice time, Grant?"

He grimaced. "Leida has introduced me to everyone here—and I'm assuming that she is currently entertaining half the population of Springfield—calling me her 'dear little brother.' I'm going to strangle her."

Merry laughed, then wished she hadn't when her head pounded a protest at the exertion. "She's only teasing you, Grant."

"I know. I'm not mad, but I *will* get even." He reached out to run a finger along her white lei, allowing his knuckles to graze her breast in the process. "I've missed you today."

Controlling her breathing with an effort, she firmly took his hand and held it well away from her bustline. "I've been right here."

"Yes, but you've been too busy to talk to me."

"I have some time now. Want something to eat?"

He shook his head, the sun catching the gold in his hair and causing it to glitter richly. "No, but I'd love a fruit drink. How about you?"

"Sounds good."

"I'll get it. Be right back." He started toward the bar, then turned back with a boyish grin. "Don't move!" he warned her.

"I won't," she promised, her heart turning over at his beautiful smile. Lord, how she loved him.

Leaning back against the low brick wall that separated Leida's pool area from her prized rose garden, Merry closed her eyes for a moment and wished for a Tylenol. She really wasn't feeling very well, she thought again. She hoped she wasn't coming down with a cold. MerryMakers had a full schedule for the next few weeks and a cold would slow her down.

"What's wrong?"

Grant's question, spoken with concern, brought her eyelids quickly back up. She forced another smile. "You were quick."

He handed her the fruit drink he'd brought her. "I was afraid you'd get away again if I wasn't. Now answer my question. What's wrong?"

She shook her head disparagingly and sipped her drink, dodging the tiny umbrella. "Nothing. Just a bit of a headache."

"Would you like to go inside and lie down for a while? You're rather pale."

"Don't be silly, Grant, it's just a headache. It'll go away on its own in a few minutes."

He searched her face, still not reassured. "Let me know if you change your mind."

"I will. I like your nephew, Grant," she added quickly, determined to change the subject before he forced her to admit just how bad she felt.

His expression cleared. "Chip? Yeah, he's a good kid. Have you noticed the way he's been looking at Meaghan?"

Merry chuckled and glanced at the group of some fifteen teenagers who were gathered in one corner of the lawn. Melinda seemed to be trying to get Savage to attempt a hula while the less extroverted Meaghan was conversing quietly with Chip Carmichael. Boyd stood slightly aloof from the crowd, glaring at Meaghan. "Maybe she's finally realized just how boring Boyd is," Merry murmured.

"Could be," Grant agreed with humor. "If you ask me, I think the main reason she's been seeing Boyd is because he's a direct opposite of Savage. Meaghan may be getting a bit tired of being known as Melinda's twin. Maybe she's trying to develop her own style."

Struck by the logic of his words, Merry nodded. "You know, you may be right. Meaghan's always been quieter than Melinda and I guess sometimes she gets overlooked because of it."

"Why do they always dress alike?" Grant asked hesitantly, as if he disapproved of the practice but was a little wary about coming right out and saying so. After all, Merry had put him quite firmly in his place once for attempting to interfere with the twins.

"It was something Mom started when they were babies," Merry admitted ruefully. "By the time she died, it was a habit that neither I nor the twins saw a need to break. I've been thinking that I should start encouraging them to dress differently sometimes."

"Could be. They do look cute, though, in those matching muumuu things."

"You really do like the twins, don't you, Grant?" Merry asked thoughtfully, studying the smile he wore as he looked across the lawn with almost brotherly affection.

He looked surprised that she would even ask. "I love them," he answered simply.

Holding her tumbler in her left hand, Merry reached up with her right to stroke Grant's cheek. "You're a very special man, Grant Bryant," she told him softly.

10

HIS EYES GLOWING with a sudden inner fire, Grant captured her hand to press it against his lips. "I'm a very lucky man," he murmured. "I'm in love with a beautiful, fascinating woman who comes equipped with a close, charming family. What more could I ask for?"

"A little more privacy?" Merry suggested, striving to lighten the mood before she burst into tears and threw herself into his arms.

"I'll take whatever I can get."

She laughed softly. "Don't try to sell me that humble routine," she accused him. "Somehow it just doesn't work, coming from you."

"No go, huh?" He grinned and leaned forward to drop a kiss on her forehead. "Just can't fool you, can I, love?"

And then he frowned. "Merry, you feel awfully warm. Are you sure you—"

Merry sighed loudly. "Grant, I've been standing outside in the sun. Of course I feel warm. Now if you'll excuse me, I'm going to go check on the Hawaiian dancers. It's almost time for them to begin."

"Where'd you find Hawaiian dancers in Missouri, anyway?"

"They're a brother and two sisters of Hawaiian ancestry whose father is on the faculty of Southwest Missouri State University. They're very good."

Grant slipped his arms around her waist. "I'd still like to turn this luau into an engagement party. What do you say, Merry? Want to make an announcement before the hula lessons begin?"

The little guy with the jackhammer pounding her skull stepped up his pace. Merry managed not to wince and grab her temples, but it wasn't easy. Her fingers tightened around the plastic tumbler in her hand as she decided to keep up the light tone. "And draw attention away from the dancers your sister is paying good money for? We couldn't do that, Grant."

He smiled, accepting her diversion for what it was, but she saw the disappointment that he couldn't quite hide. "I guess you're right. If we wait until another time, Leida will have an excuse to throw another party. See, love, I'm learning patience."

"If you say so," she answered with unconcealed skepticism, earning a chuckle from him. Relieved that another potentially tense moment had passed, she excused herself to go see to the entertainment.

Just under an hour later the little man in her head had augmented his jackhammering with periodic blasts of some powerful explosive. Hoping her smile looked less sickly than it felt, Merry watched the laughing antics of Leida's guests as they participated eagerly in the lighthearted hula lessons.

"Merry, have you seen Grant?" Leida asked from close by.

Barely managing not to wince as she turned her head toward Leida, setting off another blast at her right temple, Merry moistened her lips with her tongue and tried to speak coherently. "No, I haven't seen him in almost an hour. I was just wondering where he'd gotten to."

"He and Tim sneaked off, darn them. Is it asking too much to expect the guest of honor to stay until the party's over?"

Merry frowned in surprise. Grant hadn't said anything to her about leaving the party. She was surprised that he had. "Sorry, Leida, I don't know where he is. I'm sure he'll be back soon."

"Merry, are you okay?" Marsha asked worriedly, appearing suddenly in front of her after Leida had drifted away to look for Grant and Tim. "You look—"

"Yes, I know. I look pale," Merry finished in resignation. "I'm okay, Marsh. It's just another headache."

"Grant asked me to keep an eye on you when he left. He was worried about you."

"When he left? Where'd he go?"

Marsha shrugged. "I don't know. He and Tim said they had an errand to run. They left about a half an hour ago. They were very mysterious about it."

"How strange," Merry mused, chewing her lower lip.

"I thought so, too. Why don't you go lie down for a while? I can handle this out here."

"That's not necessary, Marsha. Really. But thanks. If it gets any worse, I promise I'll do something."

"Okay, if you're sure," Marsha conceded reluctantly.

"I'm sure. Check the buffet table, will you? There's more fruit in the kitchen if we need it."

With a last worried look at her sister, Marsha complied, though she didn't look too happy about doing so.

"Need help with anything, Merry?" Meaghan asked a few minutes later.

"No, I don't think so. Are you having a good time?" Merry managed to ask lightly.

Meaghan nodded. "Yeah. Chip's been showing me his carvings. He's very good. You should see the cigar store Indian that he carved. It's about six inches high, and it looks so real you won't believe he did it himself."

"I'd love to see it. But where's Boyd?" Merry asked carefully.

Meaghan lifted her chin in annoyance. "He left almost an hour ago. He's hacked off because I've been talking to Chip. I don't think I'll be going out with him anymore. I'm fed up with his moods."

Knowing that Meaghan had been quite captivated by Boyd at one time, Merry frowned in concern. "Are you okay, Meaghan?"

"Yeah, I'm okay. It's just all so confusing, isn't it? Does it get easier to understand guys when you get older, Merry?"

Merry chuckled softly and gave her sister a quick hug. "No, honey, it doesn't get any easier. I wish I could tell you it does."

"Oh, well," Meaghan sighed, pulling away with a rueful smile. "Life goes on. I think I'll go look at Chip's Indian again."

"You do that." Merry watched with a touch of envy as her sister walked away. Despite the melodrama, it *was* easier to be a teenager than a supposedly mature adult, she decided.

Where was Grant? She glanced around at the dwindling crowd of guests, hoping to spot his golden-brown head or colorful shirt. She was hit by a sudden urge to be with him, to tell him how bad she felt and soak up his sympathy. Her throbbing temples craved his soothing massage.

She needed him. She loved him and she needed him. And all she had to do was say yes and she'd be engaged to him, even married to him. He wanted it. She wanted it. So what was holding her back?

Fear.

She couldn't deal with her complicated feelings for Grant just then. Not in addition to the headache that was making dark-centered circles of light whirl crazily in front of her eyes.

She swallowed a moan, realizing that she was about to embarrass herself by passing out in front of Leida's guests and desperate to prevent it. Groping blindly for the tree where she stood, she turned her head in search of one of her sisters, knowing she needed help to make it to the house. She only hoped they could manage the feat discreetly.

As if he sensed something wrong, Savage looked up from where he stood talking to Melinda a few yards away. His eyes met Merry's and then he was moving, bolting toward her as she swayed. "Merry?" he asked worriedly, catching her forearms in his strong hands. "You okay?"

"I feel lousy, Savage," she whispered, leaning into him. "I think I'm going to have to leave the party."

He slipped a supportive arm around her shoulders. "Come on. I'll take you home. Your crew can take care of everything here. You certainly have enough people working this party."

"Merry?" Marsha and the twins gathered around their sister in concern. "What's wrong?"

"Just this terrible headache," Merry answered in what she hoped was a reassuring tone. "Savage is going to take me home. Marsha—"

"I'll look after things here," Marsha assured her. "Unless you need me to go with you . . . ?"

"No, thanks. I'd rather you'd stay."

"I'm going with you," Melinda announced defiantly.

Merry didn't feel like arguing. Anxious to leave without further explanations, she allowed Melinda and Sav-

age to bustle her to his Mustang. Savage helped her in
solicitously, watching as she dropped her head against
the back of the seat with a moan, her eyes closing wearily. "I think we'll make a stop by the clinic on the way to
your house," he told her, climbing behind the wheel.

"No, Savage, that's not—"

"It's no trouble at all," he broke in, though he knew full
well that she wasn't concerned about that. "Besides," he
added with a note of humor lurking beneath the concern in his voice, "I'm driving."

Merry wondered why she'd never noticed before that
Savage and Grant had a lot in common.

"GRANT, MY MAN, when you're right, you're right!"
Tim proclaimed enthusiastically, slapping his friend on
the back as they made their way toward Leida's front
door. "How'd you know for sure he was behind the robberies?"

Grant shrugged modestly. "He was the only suspect I
didn't like," he admitted, making no claim to scientific
reasoning. "I'm just glad we talked Sheriff Roland into
going along with our plan today—and that our plan
worked!"

"Me too. Merry and Marsha will be so relieved to get
this behind them. I just hope they're not too upset when
they find out who's been behind the robberies."

"They won't be," Grant predicted, though he wasn't
so sure how another member of the family would react.
He twisted the front doorknob, glancing around the
driveway as he did so. "Looks like the party's beginning
to break up. We've been gone for over an hour, so I guess
it's not surprising that some people have already left.
Leida may be ready to have my hide for running out on
her that way."

"She'll understand when you tell her what happened."

"Grant! Where have you been?" Leida grabbed her brother's arm the moment he stepped onto her patio. "We've been looking everywhere for you!"

"I'll tell you all about it in a few minutes," he promised, looking around for a beloved dark head. "Where's Merry?"

"Savage and Melinda took her home. She was ill."

"She's ill?" Grant grabbed his sister's arm, the color draining from his face. "What's wrong with her?"

"Marsha told me that Merry complained of a bad headache and Savage offered to drive her home. Poor dear was concerned about the party, as if I cared about the party when she's ill."

Grant was already on his way out the door, his heart pounding in his chest. Tim rushed to catch up with him. "Want me to go with you?"

Grant shook his head. "No, thanks. Stay with Marsha. They may need some help packing up the decorations," he added, forgetting for the moment that the entire crew was on hand at his request. He slammed his fist into his other hand. "Dammit, I *knew* she wasn't feeling well. I never should have left her."

"You were trying to help her," Tim reassured him as his friend climbed into the Ferrari. "You knew she'd been worried about this robbery thing and you wanted to help solve it. You did."

"I was out playing cops and robbers while she was so sick she had to leave the party," Grant refuted in self-disgust. "I didn't trust the police to handle it on their own."

"Grant, stop beating yourself up and go to her. And drive carefully," Tim warned as Grant slammed the door and gunned the engine.

Grant was fortunate that Springfield's finest were busy in other parts of town just then. He made it to Merry's house in record time, parking behind Savage's Mustang and leaping out of his own car with more haste than grace. Without bothering to knock, he entered the house, finding Savage and Melinda in the den. "Where's Merry?"

"She's sleeping," Melinda replied, not in the least surprised to see Grant in such a state. "Dr. Thomas gave her a shot of something for the headache and it's made her groggy."

"She's seen a doctor?"

"Yeah. Savage insisted that we stop by the clinic on the way home," Melinda answered with a look of pride at her boyfriend.

"What's wrong with her?"

This time it was Savage who responded to Grant's terse question. "The doc said she had the flu, complicated by stress and near exhaustion. He said it was obvious she hasn't been taking care of herself lately—too much stress, too little sleep, too much coffee. He recommended at least one full week away from the office, preferably two."

"She won't like that," Melinda predicted.

"She'll take the two weeks if I have to tie her to her bed," Grant replied grimly.

"I should have known she was about to be sick," Melinda bemoaned. "She's had so many headaches lately and she hasn't been sleeping well. I sat up with her myself for a while last night. She was really letting everything get to her."

Grant wished Merry had told him about the headaches and sleepless nights. Maybe he could have done more to help her. He couldn't stand the thought of her being ill. "I'm going in to check on her," he told the others, turning abruptly toward Merry's bedroom.

She was lying quietly, her eyes closed, her dark eyelashes contrasting dramatically with her skin, which was almost as white as the sheets. Her chocolate-brown hair was spread around her face, soft and lush. Grant reached out to stroke it, noting dispassionately that his hand was trembling. She stirred, her lashes fluttering, then opening. "Grant," she whispered.

He started to answer, then had to stop and clear his throat. "Hi, sweetheart. How do you feel?"

"Stupid," she answered in disgust. "I ruined Leida's party."

"Don't worry about Leida's party. It was very nice. You did a great job of putting it together." He placed his palm tenderly against her forehead. "Headache better?"

"Yes, the doctor gave me something for it. It's much better."

"Good." He kissed the corner of her mouth. "Guess you're going to have to slow down for a week or two. Let someone else be in charge for a while."

She sighed and closed her eyes for a moment, then opened them again. "I don't suppose I have any choice."

"I don't suppose you do."

She groped for his hand. "I'm glad you're here, Grant."

"I should have been with you all along," he muttered, raising her hand to his lips, his fingers twining with hers. "I didn't realize that you were so ill. I'm sorry."

She managed a weak smile. "Where'd you and Tim disappear to, anyway? Did you have all the party you could take?"

"No. We were out solving your robbery mystery. You don't have to worry about that anymore, love. It's taken care of. Your business won't suffer from that now."

She frowned in confusion. "Someone was arrested?"

He nodded. "Caught in the act."

"But who was it?"

He hesitated, wondering if she were up to hearing everything.

Her fingers tightened in his. "Grant, who was it?"

"Boyd," he answered finally.

Her eyes widened dramatically. *"Boyd? Are you sure?"*

"I'm sure. It seems he had a real teenage crime ring going. He'd get names and addresses from Meaghan—very smoothly, of course—and his buddies and he were hitting the homes during the parties. Tim and I followed him today when he left Leida's and caught him and two others just entering a home they had no business entering. Sheriff Roland took it from there. I'd told him that I suspected Boyd and he gave me the benefit of the doubt."

"You suspected Boyd? Why?"

"I didn't like him," Grant replied, giving the same answer he'd given Tim. After all, it was the truth.

Merry pushed a strand of hair away from her face with her free hand, blinking in disbelief. "He really had me fooled," she confessed. "I never would have suspected Boyd. I thought he was too boring to be that cunning."

"That's just what he wanted you to think."

"I wonder why he did it?"

"Who knows? I don't know about his family life, but it could be that he needed money for drugs or something. Or maybe he just did it for kicks."

"And the police suspected Savage because he dresses oddly and wears earrings," Merry said indignantly. And then she frowned. "Poor Meaghan. I hope she doesn't blame herself."

"I'll talk to her," Grant promised.

"Maybe I should—"

He shook his head, knowing that she didn't like having control taken out of her hands but determined that she would get the rest her doctor had ordered. "She probably already knows by now. I'm sure Tim had told the others what happened. You're not up to a long heart-to-heart tonight."

"I wish you'd stop treating me like an invalid, Grant," Merry complained. "I've only got the flu."

"Complicated by stress and exhaustion." He leaned over her, stroking her hair, his gaze meeting hers intently. "Merry, it's just what I've been telling you. You try to do too much and you spend too much time worrying about others and not enough on yourself. I—" He stopped and swallowed, then continued, "I haven't helped you by pressuring you into a relationship you weren't ready for. You asked for time, but I just kept rushing you. I'm sorry, Merry."

"No, Grant, I—"

He shushed her by placing two fingers over her mouth. "It's okay, Merry. I'm only promising not to rush you anymore. We'll slow down and we'll take our relationship one step at a time. Whatever you're comfortable with. I won't push you into an engagement or marriage, nor will I pressure you for more of your time. If you can learn to take better care of yourself, I can learn patience. It won't be easy for either of us, but we'll manage. I know we will."

She shook her head, tangling her hair against the pillow. "Grant," she murmured, her voice muffled beneath his fingers, "I—"

Whatever she'd planned to say was lost when Marsha joined them, tiptoeing with exaggerated care to Merry's bedside. "Merry, are you all right?"

"I'll go now and let you get your rest," Grant said before Merry could answer. "Take care of yourself, love."

"But, Grant, I—"

Again his fingers stopped her words. "I love you," he murmured, then made himself leave her while he still could. He leaned for a moment against the wall in the hallway, picturing her again so pale and sick. He couldn't stand the thought of Merry's being in pain. Nor the guilt that swamped him as he wondered if he had contributed to her illness. He was determined that she would have no further stress from him. Then he straightened and steeled himself to talk to Meaghan about Boyd.

MERRY GLARED AT THE DOOR that had closed behind her exasperating lover. She hadn't wanted him to leave. She'd wanted him to stay with her, but he'd refused to allow her to tell him so. Why wouldn't that man ever listen to her?

"How do you feel, Merry?"

Turning her gaze to Marsha, Merry moistened her lips. "Like I've been dragged behind a car. Other than that, I'm fine."

Marsha chuckled and patted her sister's hand. "Yeah, that's about the way I felt when I was down with the flu. Miserable, isn't it?"

"Yeah." Merry closed her eyes for a few moments, feeling sleep creeping up on her. She wondered how long the medication she'd been given to dull her headache would make her so sleepy.

"Do you need me to get you anything before I leave you to rest?" Marsha asked solicitously.

"No, thanks."

"Melinda told me that Dr. Thomas recommended two weeks off work. I think you should take it if he thinks it's best for you."

Everyone knew what was best for her, Merry thought disgruntledly. "I'm sure I'll be fine in a couple of days. I should be back at work by—"

"Two weeks. Not one day before."

Merry blinked at the force behind her sister's words. When had meek, sweet-natured Marsha learned to sound so firm? "That's ridiculous. A week at the most."

"Dr. Thomas said two weeks and you're taking two weeks, my dear sister. Even if we have to accept Grant's offer to tie you to your bed. At least, that's what Savage and Melinda told me he said." A thread of humor laced Marsha's voice now.

Scowling, Merry pushed out her lower lip in a gesture she hadn't used since she was ten. "He wouldn't dare."

Marsha laughed. "I think you know him better than that. Seriously, Merry, you need this time off. Don't worry about the business."

"How can I not worry about it?" Merry demanded. "I can't possibly take off two full weeks! It would be disastrous."

Marsha James didn't get angry very often, but when she did, she could inject pure ice into her voice. "Thanks a lot, Merry, for your vote of confidence."

"Marsha, I didn't mean—"

"Did *I* automatically assume that the business would go under when *I* had the flu? Didn't I trust you to know what you were doing? I've been working at your side in that business since the day it opened, Merry Kathleen James, and I'm perfectly capable of running it for two weeks without you. Now since you're ill, I'm going to pretend you didn't say what you said, or we'll get into the kind of fight we used to have when we were teenagers and we had to share a room. I think you'd better get some rest now."

Merry groaned and slid lower in the bed after Marsha had left the room. Oh, great, she thought ruefully. She'd made her sister mad. And, she added with a sudden flash of perception, Marsha had been completely justified in being angry. Merry *had* acted as if the business would fall apart without her.

It seemed that Grant had been right about many things. Merry had been the head of the family and the leader at the office for so long that she'd lost the ability to delegate, to trust the capabilities of others. How incredibly arrogant she'd been, she thought, even as she gave up trying to hold off sleep and allowed herself to slip into blessed oblivion

THE NEXT FEW DAYS WERE among the most frustrating of Merry's life. After the first four days of feeling completely miserable, feverish and aching and ill, she began to recuperate, and restlessness immediately set in. She wasn't accustomed to inactivity, and it wasn't as easy as it had sounded to suddenly relinquish all responsibility. And to make it worse, her family was treating her like glass, carefully protecting her from anything they deemed at all stressful.

"How's it going at school, Melinda?" she asked her sister at breakfast on Friday, the first day she'd been allowed to join the others at the table.

"It's going fine, Merry," Melinda answered carelessly, tossing her hair over the shoulder of her electric-blue T-shirt and reaching for a biscuit. "No probs."

"What about your math class? Do you think you've brought your grade up?"

"Yeah, I have. Grant's been helping me with it. He's pretty sharp with that kind of thing."

"Oh." Disconcerted, Merry fell quiet. So Grant had been helping Melinda with her homework, had he? He certainly hadn't been spending any time with Merry. He'd rationed out his visits to her during the past week as if he expected her to charge him for his time, telling her that he didn't want to overtire her. He'd called every day, but she'd seen him alone only once since Saturday and that had been a most unsatisfactory visit, with him sitting all the way across the room making innocuous small talk guaranteed not to cause her any stress. By the time he'd left, she'd wanted to strangle him.

She turned to Meaghan. "How about you, kid? Doing okay?"

Meaghan nodded, straightening the collar of her green-and-white plaid top as she did so. Probably at a suggestion from Grant, the twins had begun to dress differently at times; today was one of those days. "Just fine, Merry. Did I tell you that Boyd's scheduled for a hearing next week? Rumor has it that he'll be sent to a juvenile facility for a while."

"How do you feel about that?"

"I was pretty bummed out at first," Meaghan admitted with a shrug. "I felt guilty—like I should have known what was going on all the time. But Grant told me that Boyd had everyone else fooled, too, so I shouldn't feel so bad. We talked for a long time. And I've got a date with Chip for the end-of-school dance next week."

Grant, again. He had time for everyone but her lately, Merry thought. She shot a sideways glance at Marsha, who was finishing her coffee with a secretive smile. "I suppose Grant's helping out at the office, too?" she asked a little too sweetly.

Marsha made a not-quite-successful effort to hide a smile as she answered. "He and Tim have been busy starting up their own new business. I think they'll be very successful with their computer consulting firm, especially with their impressive background in the field. Tim's pretty excited about it; he's particularly interested in working with small companies that are just beginning to computerize. They've found an office not far from ours and they've ordered some equipment. But they've both been by a few times this week to see if there was anything they could do."

"Wasn't that nice of them." Merry spoke without enthusiasm.

"He's been spending a lot of time with Chip, too," Meaghan volunteered. "Chip's just crazy about Grant."

"Aren't we all?" Merry muttered, almost to herself.

"Well, time for us to go," Marsha announced cheerfully. "See you later, Merry. Call if you need anything."

"Maybe I could come by the office later this afternoon."

Marsha shook her head, her silvery blond hair swaying emphatically. "You will not. You can still barely make it from the kitchen to your bedroom without your knees buckling. Don't you dare try to leave this house."

Merry sighed and gave in, knowing Marsha was right but resenting it, anyway. "I'm bored," she told the empty kitchen when the others had gone off to their respective destinations. "Bored, bored, bored!"

But no one was there to care.

Grant called her later that morning. "How're you doing, love?"

"I'm bored, Grant. I'm going to start screaming if I don't get out of this house soon," she warned him.

"Anyone ever tell you that you're a terrible patient, Merry?"

"Don't you dare laugh at me!"

"I'm not laughing," he told her, though he was obviously lying through his chuckles. "Tell you what. If you're a very good girl, I'll take you for a drive this weekend. Maybe I'll even buy you an ice-cream cone."

Merry told him quite clearly what he could do with his ice-cream cone, sending him into a fresh peal of laughter.

"Can't you come over this afternoon?" Merry asked him wistfully, wanting desperately to be alone with him. Her palms itched to touch him, and her lips hungered for his. It had been so long since they'd been together.

"I'd love to, honey, but Tim and I have an appointment with a potential client for Bryant and Castle Consulting. I'll be by later, though."

Which meant that everyone else would be home and they still wouldn't be alone. Merry sighed. "Good luck with your appointment."

"Thanks. Get some rest now, okay?"

Any more rest and she'd turn into a feather pillow, she thought as she hung up the phone. She was struck by the irony of the situation. It seemed that she and Grant had reversed roles somehow. Now it was Grant who was busy with his career and Merry trying to wheedle a bit of his time. She moistened suddenly dry lips with her tongue, wondering if her fears that Grant would lose interest in her once he found something else to do were beginning to come true.

GRANT DID take Merry out for ice cream on Sunday.
They were joined by Tim, Marsha, Chip and the twins.
They took Merry's car since it was large enough—well,
almost large enough—to hold all seven of them. Tim,
Marsha and Melinda sat in the front, with Merry, Grant,
Meaghan and Chip in the back. It felt wonderful to be out
again and Merry truly enjoyed the outing, but sitting so
close to Grant was just short of torture. It seemed like
months since they'd made love, and her rapidly
strengthening body was reminding her that she had other
needs besides food and rest. She wondered how he could
sit so calmly beside her, seemingly unaffected by her
proximity. Didn't he still want her?

That question was answered soon after they returned
home, when Merry found herself unexpectedly alone
with Grant in the kitchen for a few precious minutes.
With no warning he crowded her up against the wall,
trapping her there with a hand on either side of her, and
kissed her until she was trembling and breathless. And
since they were pressed intimately together from chest
to knee, she no longer had to ask herself whether Grant
still wanted her. He did.

"I thought I was going to go crazy in that car," he
muttered into her hair when he paused for an oxygen
break. "Every time you wiggled, I almost swallowed my
tongue. And you weren't helping by rubbing your leg
against mine every chance you got."

She wrapped her arms around his neck and hugged him. "I was beginning to wonder if you were made of stone. I was melting all over the upholstery, and you were just sitting there looking distant."

He'd developed an intense interest in the shape of her earlobe. He traced it slowly with the tip of his tongue. "Mmm. This tastes better than ice cream."

She laughed breathlessly and snuggled closer. "Want to make a trip to the office?"

"Oh, Merry," he groaned. "If I thought you were up to it..."

Just as she was about to convince him that she was indeed up to it, the kitchen was invaded by two hungry James teenagers who declared that the ice cream had only whetted their healthy appetites. Shortly afterward Grant claimed he had some paperwork to do to prepare for an early-morning meeting.

Merry lay awake for a long time that night, finally coming to the conclusion that she liked it better when Grant was rushing her than when he was being so damned noble.

The family began to treat her more normally the second week, accepting that she was over her flu, but still refusing to allow her to return to work. She spent her days reading and practicing her guitar. She attended her guitar class on Tuesday night and went shopping for a couple of hours with a friend on Wednesday. Merry and Marsha spent a pleasant hour working at home on Wednesday night, double-checking the arrangements for a large, Western-theme party to be held Friday evening. Merry complimented Marsha on the work she'd done during the past week, admitting that Marsha was as capable as her sister of running the business.

"I know," Marsha replied, pleased with the praise. "But, Lord, I'll be glad when you're back!" she added with a laugh.

By Thursday Merry had had enough. Everyone but Grant had finally stopped treating her like an invalid. She was feeling perfectly well again and determined to confront Grant about his ridiculous efforts to give her time—time she no longer wanted. When he called her at noon to check on her, she was ready for him.

"I'm fine . . . I guess," she told him in answer to his inquiry, deliberately making her voice thin and wistful.

Immediately picking up his cue, he demanded, "What's wrong? Are you feeling ill again?"

"Not ill, exactly," she prevaricated, the fingers of her free hands crossed behind her back.

"I'll be right there," he told her, hanging up with enough haste to leave her ears ringing.

Merry laughed and reached for her hairbrush, knowing Grant was likely to throttle her when he arrived to find her well and healthy, but equally confident that she could make him forget his annoyance.

GRANT CLIMBED OUT of his car and slammed the door behind him, his long strides taking him rapidly toward Merry's front door. There'd been something in her voice when he'd talked to her that had made him uncomfortable. Something that had drawn him to her.

He hoped she wasn't ill again. She'd seemed so much better. He'd certainly been giving her plenty of time to recuperate. Staying away from her as much as he had for the past week and a half had been driving him slowly insane. If he hadn't kept himself busy with Bryant and Castle Consulting, he wouldn't have been able to stay away from her as much as he had. But he was determined not to rush her anymore. He still felt guilty about her collapse, knowing that his pressuring her to marry him on less than two weeks' acquaintance had been part of the stress she'd been under.

He started to ring the bell, then on impulse tried the doorknob instead. The door wasn't locked. He slipped inside the house, walking quietly in the direction of Merry's bedroom. He didn't want to startle her, but if she were sleeping, he didn't want to waken her, either.

"It's about time you got here," she told him, sitting on the edge of her bed in a clinging silk robe the color of cotton candy. Looking at him with her huge green eyes, she gave him a smile that lodged itself in his windpipe.

Bracing himself with one hand on the doorjamb, he stared at her. Lord, she was beautiful. "You're, uh..." He stopped to clear his throat. "You're not ill?"

She stood in one smooth, sinuous movement, the candy-pink robe slithering against her legs. "I have this terrible ache," she told him, her voice pure seduction.

He was strangling. He loosened his tie, still holding on to the door with his other hand. "You do? Where?"

Her hands went to the knot of the sash that closed her robe. "All over. I think I know what it is, though," she added, thoughtfully, toying with that knot.

His eyes focused in fascination on her restless fingers. "What?"

"I spend too much time worrying." The knot loosened, allowing the sash to fall to either side of her. "Too much time weighing consequences, taking care of others." The robe slipped off her shoulders and cascaded to the floor, leaving her clad only in a silk-and-lace teddy of the same delectable color.

His gaze falling to her slender legs, Grant swallowed hard.

"Not enough time doing what *I* want," she continued quietly. One shoulder dipped and a frivolously thin strap fell to hang enticingly on her upper arm. The lacy top of the teddy just covered the tips of her breasts, leaving the milky-soft upper slopes bare. He could see the dark rose nipples through the sheer fabric, noting in pleasure that they were already beginning to harden. As he was.

"What do you think of my self-diagnosis, Grant?"

She'd reduced him to a blithering idiot, he thought, but he made a valiant effort to keep her from knowing it. "That's what I've been telling you all along."

"Yes, it is, isn't it?" She took two steps forward, watching him from beneath her lush, dark lashes. "Know what I've decided to do?"

The expression on his face probably told her that he not only knew what she'd decided but heartily approved. Still, he kept the game going, eager to see what she'd do next. "What's that?"

"I've decided to reward myself for being such a good patient for the past week and a half," she told him, her hands sliding up his chest to stop at his loosened tie. She deftly removed it. "I've decided not to worry about MerryMakers or my family for an hour or so. I'm not even going to worry about whether I'm keeping you from something you need to do. I'm going to be totally selfish." By the time she finished that speech, she had his shirt unbuttoned and pulled from the waistband of his dark blue suit pants.

"What do you think?" she inquired mildly, her hand skimming the evidence of his intense interest in her little performance.

"I think you know what's best for you," he told her a bit hoarsely, shrugging out of his jacket and shirt in one jerky movement and allowing them to fall unheeded to the floor.

Her smile was blissful as she took advantage of his actions to spread her palms across his rapidly rising and falling chest, her fingertips encircling his nipples. "Yes, I know what's best for me, Grant. You. You're best for me."

"Oh, God, Merry." He'd had about all he could take of her erotic taunting. There'd been too many long, lonely nights and unsuccessful cold showers since the last time he'd made love with her. He was on fire for her, every nerve in his hard, aroused body thrumming with need. His hands clenched into white-knuckled fists. "You're making it very hard for me to remember that you've been ill."

"Grant." She rose onto her toes to press her mouth lightly to his, her hands cupping his face. "Make love with me. Please. I need you."

Something snapped inside him. His arms went around her in a crushing embrace, forcing him to loosen them before her hurt her. He buried his face in the soft curve of her neck, inhaling deeply the sultry scent she'd worn for him. "I love you," he muttered thickly, his hands caressing her scantily clad curves with near desperation. "God, how I love you."

"Grant, I—"

But he could wait no longer to kiss her. His mouth came down hard on hers, blocking whatever she might have said. The kiss was deep and hungry, drawing them into it until their entire world was reduced to two bodies, two heartbeats. Grant burned with the need to be one.

It took only a flick of his trembling fingers to have the teddy at her feet. "You are so beautiful," he murmured, stroking her lightly from throat to thigh. "So very beautiful."

Merry stood proudly before him, emboldened by his praise. "So are you," she assured him in an unsteady voice, reaching for the snap of his slacks. He helped her so that it was only a matter of moments before they stood naked together.

His hands on her hips, he drew her forward until they were pressed against each other. His eyes closed as the breath shuddered out of him. Sweat beaded on his forehead, and he hoped he'd have the strength to retain control over himself. He wanted to make this so very good for her.

He groaned when Merry's caressing hands slipped between them to stroke him intimately. With a ragged laugh he caught her wrists and lifted her hands away from him. "Touch me now," he told her in an answer to the question in her passion-darkened green eyes, "and this will be over before we get to the bed."

She looked startled, then pleased.

"Proud of yourself, aren't you?" he asked indulgently, eyeing her utterly feminine smile. "You like knowing you have the power to reduce me to the same level as an awkward, oversexed teenager."

Her husky chuckle was his undoing. He snatched her into his arms and tumbled her unceremoniously on the bed, determined to pay her back with interest for the pleasure-misery she'd just put him through. Breathless and laughing, Merry squirmed beneath him, further arousing him with the friction of skin against skin. Her laughter became a moan when he kissed her again, arching against her in a pale imitation of what they both knew would follow.

"Oh, Grant, I want you so much." Her throaty whisper coursed over him in much the same manner as her exploring hands. Her palms slid over his shoulders to dip in at his waist and then caress his buttocks, causing tiny electric shocks along their path.

"I've been going crazy wanting you," he groaned in response, his mouth seeking and finding one nipple. His tongue circled it, then drew it deep into his mouth. Merry cried out and arched upward, her hands clenching in his hair. Reveling in her responsiveness, he slid his fingers downward, over the gentle slope of her stomach to the tangle of dark curls below. He found her so hot and damp and ready that he had to stop and pull in a long, sharp breath to steady himself. His first impulse was to plunge deeply inside that waiting softness, but he knew if he did, the lovemaking would be over almost immediately.

"Not yet," he muttered, more to himself than her. "Not yet."

He stroked her lovingly, at the same time touching just the edge of his teeth to her breast. She whispered his name, lifting herself pleadingly into his touch. The moan she made when he slipped a finger deep inside her was the most beautiful sound he'd ever heard. She tightened around him, incoherently pleading for more.

His own body demanded release, but Grant held back, wanting to watch her find her pleasure before he succumbed to his own. His hands continued to stroke her, rubbing and gliding as his lips sought the sensitive hollows of her throat and behind her ear. His tongue laved her, leaving damp, glistening patches to mark where he'd been. His teeth nipped delicately, tearing delighted little cries from her throat. He rubbed himself against her silky thigh, knowing he couldn't hold out much longer.

"Grant! Oh, please, Grant, I don't think I can stand any more," she said, gasping, echoing his own thoughts. She bowed sharply upward when his thumb found the ultrasensitive nub of her femininity.

"That's it, love. Let go. Just let go." He drove her harder, faster, his narrowed eyes intent on the expression crossing her flushed face. His thumb moved again, and she convulsed beneath his hand, her eyes squeezing shut as wave upon wave of pleasure rippled almost visibly through her.

Only when she'd experienced the full measure of her climax did Grant give in to his own need. Covering her quivering lips with his, he entered her. Her arms and legs closed welcomingly around him, her breathlessly musical voice urging him on with tender endearments. He closed his eyes and thrust mindlessly, hoarsely shouting her name as release exploded inside him.

Cradling her in his arms, he drifted, mind and body sated with her, knowing he would want her again and again and again—for the rest of his life. Words trembled on his tongue—pleas for her to love him, to marry him, to be with him always—but he swallowed them, his arms tightening around her. It would happen when she was ready. He couldn't bear to consider otherwise.

"I think I'm feeling better," Merry mused aloud, laughter in her voice. "That was just what I needed."

Grant chuckled and lifted his head. "You little witch. I thought you'd had a relapse. Now I find it hard to believe you've been ill at all."

"Finally." She twisted until she was smiling down into his face, her hands linked behind his neck. "I was forced to take drastic measures to convince you that I'm perfectly healthy now."

"I'm not complaining about your drastic measures. I'm delighted that you're healthy. I want you to stay that way."

"Does that mean I can count on you for more of your special TLC?" she asked provocatively, dropping a kiss on his jaw.

"Anytime, love," he answered without hesitation.

Merry dropped her head to his chest and snuggled against him, feeling deliciously limp and lethargic, thoroughly pleased with her first attempt at outright seduction. It had worked so well this time that she would have to try it again, she decided with a slight smile. Many times. But only with Grant. There was no one else she wanted to seduce—not now, not ever.

There were so many things she wanted to say to him. So much she'd learned since he'd stormed into her life. Primarily that she wanted him to stay in her life. For always.

She'd tell him what she was thinking in a moment, she thought sleepily, contentedly. She'd tell him how much she loved him. That she was ready to talk about a commitment, a future, if not to actually walk down the aisle. She closed her eyes and nestled deeper into his warm, damp shoulder. She'd tell him in a moment, she thought again, then promptly fell asleep.

Grant smiled tenderly, holding her close to his heart while she slept. He stroked her hair lightly, careful not to wake her. He'd allow her to sleep for a short time, he decided, then he'd rouse her when it was time for him to go. He closed his eyes and lay still, luxuriating in the warm feel and fresh scent of her.

Sometime later Grant stirred, frowned, opened his eyes and lifted his left arm from Merry's shoulders to check the time on his watch. "Damn! Merry, wake up!"

He shook her gently, easing himself out from under her at the same time.

Blinking sleepy eyes, Merry groaned and pushed her hair out of her face. "What's wrong, Grant?"

"Your family will be here at any minute. We're just damned lucky I woke up when I did," he answered, scrambling into his clothes. He draped his tie around the collar of his partially buttoned shirt and groped on the floor. "Dammit, where are my socks?"

Merry laughed. "You act like a teenager about to get caught by his girlfriend's father," she accused him, reaching for the pair of jeans and knit top she'd worn earlier that day—before she'd changed into her seduction costume.

"I suppose it wouldn't bother you at all for your little sisters to catch us in bed together?" He sat on the edge of the bed to tug on his newly found socks.

"Of course it would. But they didn't, so relax."

Grant tucked in his shirt and looked in her dresser mirror to knot his tie. "We got lucky."

She wondered at his suddenly distant mood. Had it bothered him that much to fall asleep? she wondered as she straightened her top over her jeans. She'd have to admit that the thought of her little sisters finding her in bed with Grant made her very uncomfortable, but she wasn't overreacting to the near miss, as he was. She wasn't sure it was the right time to discuss the future with him, but she made a feeble effort, anyway. "Grant, about the house you like in Cinnamon Square—"

He turned his head to look at her, opened his mouth to speak, then stopped as the sound of car doors slamming in the driveway outside drifted into the room. "The kids are home," he announced unnecessarily. He shoved his fingers through his hair, restoring it to a semblance of its usual casual style.

Merry quickly brushed her hair, then set the brush back on the dresser and turned to Grant, who'd straightened the bed, opened the bedroom door and stood leaning against the doorjamb as if he hadn't even been inside. She found herself resenting that pose, resenting that neither of them felt he had the right to be found in her bedroom, resenting the emotional distance he'd suddenly put between them. Why couldn't he have seen the humor in the situation? They could be sharing a laugh with their eyes; instead, he looked as if he were angry with her for the awkwardness of the past few minutes.

"Grant, we really do need to talk," she ventured carefully.

"Later," he replied, just as a chattering twin in vivid red appeared and grabbed hold of his arm.

"Grant! Hi, guess what?" She continued without allowing him time to make a guess. "I got an A on my math test! Whizzed right through those word problems. Thanks for helping me study."

"You're welcome, Melinda, and congratulations. I knew you were ready for the test."

"Hey, Grant," another strawberry blonde, this one dressed in yellow and orange, chided with a teasing grin. "You're not supposed to be here. No boys in the bedrooms, right, Merry?"

"Right," Merry answered hollowly. Somehow she knew she wouldn't be alone with Grant again that evening. He, as well as her innocently intrusive family, would see to it.

She was right. He left a couple of hours later, giving her nothing more than a quick kiss on the cheek. Merry felt like throwing something at him as he left. Preferably herself.

MUTTERING UNDER his breath, Grant prowled restlessly through the tastefully, if unspectacularly, furnished apartment that Tim had rented a few days before. Tim watched for a time in amused silence before finally speaking up. "You do realize, don't you, that you're wearing a path in my new carpet?"

Grant scowled down at the plush fabric beneath his feet. "I don't care for the color, anyway. You don't strike me as the type to have pink carpet in your apartment."

Unperturbed, Tim shrugged. "Can't say that pink is my favorite color, either, but I like the rest of the apartment okay, and it *is* furnished. Besides, Marsha called the color dusty rose."

"It's still pink."

"It'll look more my style when I bring in the things I've decided to keep from Colorado. Once I've lived here awhile, you won't be able to *see* the carpet."

Grant gave a reluctant chuckle, knowing Tim was exaggerating.

"So," Tim continued without a pause, "want to talk about it?"

"Your pink carpet?"

"Nope. Whatever the hell is making you mope around like Camille, complaining about things like the color of my rug."

"Oh. That."

"Yeah, that. Spill it, Grant. What's wrong?"

Grant put one hand to the back of his neck and squeezed, as if that would relieve some of the tension thrumming through his entire body. His mouth twisting into a wry grimace, he slanted a look at his friend. "I think I'm finally learning some of the facts of life, Tim. And I'm having a hard time dealing with them."

"Such as?"

"Such as . . ." Grant dropped his hand and threw himself into an armchair. Drawing a deep breath, he shook his head. "Such as that life doesn't always hand us what we want on a platter. That wanting something doesn't always mean we get it. That those old truisms about being patient and taking things one step at a time and crawling before you run are probably all valid."

"Truisms you've never listened to in your life," Tim pointed out.

"Maybe I should have," Grant responded glumly.

"This is just a crazy guess, but does this have something to do with you and Merry?"

"Yeah. Dammit, Tim, why couldn't I have just let things happen naturally? The way things are supposed to happen. Why do I always have to be in such a hurry?"

Tim looked a bit confused. "I don't know what—"

Grant was already on his feet again, pacing like a caged animal. "I could've introduced myself the first time I met her. Met her a time or two after that through Leida. Asked her out on a real first date, the way real people do. Waited until our second or third date to kiss her goodnight and a lot more dates to go further than that. Dated her for . . . oh, six months, a year, before I started looking at houses with nurseries. But did I?"

Tim grinned. "Obviously not."

"No." Grant shoved his fingers through his hair and glared at the amused man on the couch as if the whole thing were Tim's fault. "I just couldn't wait to go after what I wanted. What an idiot!"

Tim had to laugh. "That's exactly the way you've always been in business. You're just having to learn now that business and romance can't be conducted in exactly the same way."

"I never carried my business tactics over into my personal life before. I certainly took my time establishing my relationship with Dolores, such as it was."

"Dolores was never all that important to you," Tim replied dismissively. "Merry is. When something—or someone—is important to you, you can't be satisfied sitting back and letting nature take its course." His grin was full of old-friend mischief. "I find it a rather endearing quality in you, actually."

Grant's response to that was short and succinct. Tim laughed.

Both of them sobered quickly. Grant continued to pace until Tim asked quietly, "So what are you going to do now?"

Grant's deep sigh echoed in the quiet room. "I'm going to sit back and let things progress as quickly—or slowly—as Merry wants them to. Or at least I'm going to try."

"But the house—"

"The house is no longer an issue."

"Just one question."

Grant lifted an inquiring eyebrow.

"What if," Tim asked carefully, "Merry doesn't *want* you to back off? From what I've seen, she's as involved in this relationship as you are."

"Then it's up to her to tell me what she wants next," Grant stated flatly. Remembering her method of demonstrating that she no longer wanted him to treat her as an invalid, he grinned. "She won't be shy if she decides she's ready for more of a commitment. She'll let me know."

"Love," Tim muttered, eloquently rolling his eyes. "It certainly is complicated, isn't it?"

"Yeah. It is." Grant waited for a moment, then turned a sly smile toward Tim. "Why don't you try it? I've always hated suffering alone."

Tim frowned. "I think *I'll* just let nature take its course."

Grant nodded his understanding, looking down at the maligned carpet as his thoughts turned wistfully back to Merry.

MERRY PRESSED HER FOOT a bit harder against the accelerator and smiled to herself as the car picked up speed. It sure felt good to be out of the house without one of her sisters along to make sure she didn't "overdo it." The driver's side window was rolled down, causing her hair to toss playfully around her face, and she'd turned the radio up to a cheerful din. She felt better than she'd felt in months.

Well, she amended with a quick, sensuous grin, she'd felt even better yesterday afternoon when her seduction of Grant had met with such glorious success. The freedom of this drive was the *second* nicest feeling she'd had in months.

She was on her way to the office, where she planned to help with the preparations for the Western-theme party that evening, even though Marsha hadn't intended Merry to return to work until Monday. But Merry knew that the college helpers were all busy studying for finals and that Tim and Grant were both helping out with the preparations today, and she intended to join them.

On impulse, she turned the car toward Cinnamon Square first. She thought she'd take another look at the house she and Grant had seen together two weeks earlier. After all, she intended to be living in it soon. She laughed softly as she realized that she was now going to have to convince Grant that she'd decided she really was ready for marriage. As he'd once asked, what were the alternatives? Somehow they seemed to have progressed beyond dating and going steady. She wanted to come home to him every night, to awake in his arms every morning. To share his problems just as he'd share hers. She wanted to marry him.

She transferred her foot from the accelerator to the brake rather too abruptly when she spotted the house—and the sign in front of it. Her head jerking from the force of her squealing stop, she glared at that sign. The one marked Sold.

Someone else had bought *her* house!

MERRY PUSHED OPEN the door marked MerryMakers, her jaw set with determination. Inside she found the usual pandemonium. Melinda was on the telephone, assuring someone that the preparations for the evening's party were proceeding according to schedule and that there was nothing to worry about. Meaghan was packing red-and-white checked tablecloths and matching paper napkins into a box to be loaded into the van along with assorted wagon wheels, rodeo banners, wooden barrels and even a pitchfork, which would serve as props. Most of those items were stacked around the reception area, waiting to be carried out.

Wearing a straw cowboy hat, Tim strolled across the room with a bag of decorations thrown over his shoulder, winking at Merry when he saw her. "Howdy, Merry. We were just about to mosey on over to the roundup site. You going along?"

"Where's Grant?" Merry demanded.

"In your office with Marsha," Meaghan answered, looking up from where she sat cross-legged on the floor. "They're running through the checklist together to make sure we haven't forgotten anything. Louis is bringing the van around. He's going to help us load up before he cuts out to study."

Merry nodded, already moving toward her office, her work temporarily taking second place in her desire to talk to—yell at, actually—Grant. "Melinda, help Meaghan and Louis load the van," she instructed quietly as Melinda recradled the telephone. "This will only take a few minutes."

Neither Marsha nor Grant looked at all surprised to see Merry. She'd stayed away from the office for longer than either of them had expected. But both were startled when she planted her small feet in an aggressive stance, doubled her fists on her slender hips, turned her blazing green eyes on Grant and almost shouted, "Are you *trying* to drive me crazy or what?"

Immediately aware that she was furious, Grant lifted a curious brow. "What have I done now?" he asked mildly.

"It's not as though your family is the only one with a romantic history, you know," she continued without making an attempt to answer his question. "*My* parents eloped six weeks after they met! Didn't they, Marsha?"

"Well, yes," Marsha responded, looking confused. "What—"

"And you're not the only one who can be impulsive!" Merry went on heatedly, still looking directly at Grant. "Ask Marsha how long I thought about opening MerryMakers before I actually started accumulating props."

"Marsha, how long—" Grant began obediently, only to be interrupted by Merry.

"About a week! The idea came to me while I was working at the Convention Bureau, and a week later I bought two pink bar stools and an old Coke box at an auction! It took me another year to actually get the business started, but I was collecting props the entire time!"

"That's very interesting," Grant ventured.

"And speaking of impulsiveness—" Merry stepped closer to him and jabbed a pink-tipped finger into his broad chest. "—do you think I made a practice of getting involved with every good-looking man who wanders into the office? Or just two days after meeting that man mmmph." She stopped only when Grant's hand firmly covered her mouth.

"Merry, before you go on to embarrass both of us, is this diatribe leading to anything in particular?" Grant asked gently.

She tugged his hand away. "You told me two weeks ago that you wanted to marry me. Have you changed your mind?" she demanded boldly.

"No, love. I haven't changed my mind."

"Then why," she began, her temper rekindling, "have you been avoiding me for the past two weeks? Why wouldn't you talk to me about us? Why did you make it necessary for me to lure you to the house and mmmph."

"Because," he answered clearly, his hand over her mouth once again, "you told me you needed time to think. You said I was rushing you."

Impatiently she pushed his hand away for the second time. "I never wanted you to completely ignore me! You've helped Melinda with her homework, Meaghan with her personal problems, Marsha with the business—but you've done little more than pat me on the head and talk about the weather!"

"What do you want, Merry?" he asked quietly.

She stared at him, remembering the evening he'd shown her the house in Cinnamon Square. He'd asked her the same question that day. She hadn't known how to answer him then. She knew now. "I want to marry you."

The smile that split his face was almost blinding. He looked toward the doorway behind her. "I told you she wouldn't be shy about telling me what she wanted—once she made up her mind, of course."

Merry turned her head to find Tim standing behind her, grinning broadly. Wincing, she turned back to find Marsha staring at her in amused fascination. Grant began to laugh. Merry covered her cheeks with her hands. "I've just made a fool of myself, haven't I?"

"Yes, love. But feel free to continue, if you like. I'm enjoying it," Grant told her.

"Me, too," Marsha announced gaily, leaning back against the desk with her arms crossed loosely in front of her. "From the very beginning, this has been the craziest courtship I've ever seen."

At a look from Grant, Tim chuckled and winked at Marsha. "Maybe we should help the twins and Louis with the loading. I think Grant and Merry might want to continue this in private."

With a show of reluctance Marsha departed, closing the office door behind her after smiling mischievously at her sister. Merry groaned and hid her face in her hands.

Still laughing softly, Grant pulled her hands away and drew her into his arms. "Want to tell me what happened just now?"

She leaned her forehead against his shoulder. "I don't know, exactly." Then she lifted her head so quickly that she bumped against his chin. "Yes, I do. Our house!"

"Our—"

"Someone bought our house in Cinnamon Square!" she told him mournfully. "While you were being such a noble gentleman and giving me all that time to make decisions, someone waltzed right in and bought our house out from under us. I loved that house, Grant!"

He pulled her closer, his cheek against her hair as he rocked her tenderly in his arms. "Did you?"

"Yes. I wanted to live there with you and the twins. I wanted to use that sweet little nursery." She sighed, snuggling deeper into his warmth.

"I bought the house, Merry."

She stiffened abruptly. "You *what*?"

He held her firmly when she would have stepped away. "I bought the house. Made an offer the day after we looked at it."

"Why?" she demanded.

He smiled. "Because I knew you loved it, just as I did. And because I fully intended to live there with you—and to make use of that sweet little nursery."

She narrowed her eyes. "You mean all that talk about giving me time was—"

"Was true," he interrupted decisively. "I did plan to give you time. But I also intended to be ready when you came to the right decision."

"You arrogant, conceited, railroading—"

It wasn't his hand that stifled her words this time. It was his mouth, hard and warm and demanding a response that she had no intention of withholding. Merry dropped her head back and twined her arms around his neck, her lips opening to his as if the kiss had been her idea all along. Groaning his pleasure with her response, Grant lifted her higher against him, eagerly deepening the kiss.

"I love you," he muttered into her mouth some time later. "God, I love you!" And he kissed her again.

Merry thought longingly of satin pillows, though she knew there would be no chance of such privacy now. "I love you, Grant Bryant," she murmured softly, pressing kisses against his firm jaw. "I don't know if I'll ever be able to keep up with you, but I love you."

He threaded his fingers deep in her hair and looked at her with glowing eyes. "You've never told me before."

"Haven't I?" she asked with a tremulous smile.

"No. Tell me again."

"I love you, Grant. I love—"

And again he silenced her. Very pleasantly.

Half-sitting on, half-leaning against the desk, he spread his denim-covered legs wide and pulled her between them, nuzzling his face into the curve of her neck. "Have I ever told you how good you smell?" he asked thickly. His tongue flicked out to touch her glistening skin, his hands cupping the curves of her bottom through her red twill slacks. "How good you taste?"

"Feel free to tell me again," she whispered, shivering in his arms.

Instead of telling her, he demonstrated, his lips tasting every inch of her skin that he could reach without actually undressing her. "I want to make love with you," he groaned moments later. "Long, slow, lazy love. And then I want to sleep with you in my arms, wake up and make love again."

She shivered at the images his words evoked. "I want that, too, Grant. But—"

"I know. There's a party tonight. And the twins have to eat." His grin was crooked but understanding.

She swallowed on a sudden surge of anxiety. "Grant, are you sure this is what you want? A ready-made family in addition to the demands of my career? You're absolutely sure?"

"I'm absolutely sure," he told her lovingly, his deep voice containing not the least hint of doubt. "I'm sure I'll find a great deal of pleasure with my ready-made family. And when we close our bedroom door, I plan to find a great deal of pleasure with my wife."

Merry went up on tiptoe to press her mouth to his. The affectionate gesture quickly changed to one of passion. Neither of them heard the polite tap on the office door, so both were startled when Tim spoke close beside them. "Uh, excuse me, you two, but Marsha needs the set of keys on the desk. I knocked, but—"

"We didn't hear you," Grant finished for him, finally releasing his hold on the woman he loved. "Guess we'd better get ready for your party tonight, love," he told her, stroking her cheek with one slightly unsteady finger.

She caught his hand and placed a quick kiss on it. "Guess so. I'm going to start advertising for an additional full-time employee. I think the company can justify the expense now, especially since Anne's moving away after she graduates from the university next week."

"That sounds like a good idea," Grant told her, aware, as she was, that this was her first step in her efforts to make more free time for him. For them.

Their eyes met and held until Tim sighed gustily and said, "Are you two going to start again, or would you like to give us a hand with decorating the ballroom where they're holding this roundup tonight? We've got everything loaded but the pitchfork and the saddle."

Grant slanted a quick, happy grin at Merry. "I'll get the saddle."

She laughed, remembering, as he was, the sensual banter they'd shared about that saddle the second time they'd made love in the office. Her eyes promised that they'd return to that subject at some more private time—as soon as they could possibly arrange it.

Epilogue

MERRY STEPPED QUIETLY behind the desk where her husband pored over a computer printout. Slipping her arms around his neck, she kissed his nape. "Hi."

He leaned back and raised his hands to squeeze her forearms affectionately. "Hi, love. How was the charity ball?"

"A few minor problems, but on the whole it was very nice. What're you doing?"

"Looking over a proposal for a potential new client. His computer system is obsolete, but he's leery about changing. Tim and I have to convince him that he really wants to change."

"You'll do it," she answered confidently. In the two years that Bryant and Castle Consulting had been in business, there had been few potential clients who hadn't been convinced by the persuasive partners. "Ready to put that away for tonight?" she asked, dropping her voice to a seductive purr.

In answer he pushed the stack of papers away and stood, turning into her arms. "Got something better to offer?"

"I just might," she replied with a smile, rising on tiptoe to kiss him.

Holding her as closely as the bulge in her middle would allow, Grant returned the kiss with eager enthusiasm. It was always this way for them. Even after almost two years of marriage, they still couldn't get enough of each other. Though neither complained about the many responsibilities inherent with their respective careers and the sixteen-year-old twins living with them in the big house in Cinnamon Square, and both looked forward to the extra little responsibility who would be joining them in about three months, they still treasured each moment of privacy they could snatch for themselves. And made the most of that time.

Grant finally broke the kiss. "Why don't we discuss your ideas in our bedroom."

"Excellent suggestion." Turning in his arms, she walked with him to the open doorway of the study.

"Grant! Would you please come look at my tape player? I think something's wrong with it. My rock tapes sound like opera!"

Grant groaned. "Couldn't I look at it tomorrow, Melinda?"

Leaning over the top of the stairway banister, Melinda looked down at the couple in the hall with a frantic expression. "But, Grant, I'm trying to do my homework! You *know* I can't do my homework without my tape player!"

"Merry." Another twin appeared in the doorway leading into the den. "Marsha's on the phone. She wants to talk to you. It's about the fitting for your matron of honor dress."

"I wish she'd believe that I'm not going to get significantly larger before next weekend. There's really no need for another fitting tomorrow."

"You'd better tell her that," Meaghan replied dryly. "She's having a case of week-before-the-wedding panic."

Grant chuckled. "Sounds familiar. I caught Tim yelling at a computer monitor this morning. He swore to me that it was deliberately withholding valuable information."

"Grant!" Melinda wailed again, leaning precariously farther over the banister.

"Melinda, you're going to fall and break your pretty neck," Grant told her in fond exasperation. He slanted an apologetic look at his wife. "I'll take care of the tape player. You take care of Marsha."

Merry nodded resignedly. "Okay. Meet you in our room later?" she asked optimistically.

"It's a date," he promised, dropping a kiss on her lips before heading up the stairs. "What's wrong with opera?" Merry heard him ask Melinda as they disappeared into her bedroom. "I *like* opera."

"Ooooh, Grant! Opera's so nerpy!"

Merry cocked an eyebrow at Meaghan as they walked together toward the telephone. "Nerpy?"

Meaghan grinned. "Melinda's new word. You'll be hearing a lot of it."

"Wonderful." Merry picked up the phone. "Hello, Marsha. *Why* do I have to try on my dress again?"

Half an hour later Grant tiptoed dramatically into the master bedroom. With all the stealth of a master spy, he turned and silently closed the door behind him, cautiously pushing the knob to lock the door. Sitting on the bed, Merry giggled. Frowning, he covered his lips with one finger. "Shh," he hissed. "Do you want the world to know we're in here *alone*?" he demanded in a stage whisper.

Still giggling, Merry shook her head. "No! If they find out, they'll try to tear us apart again."

"Right." He headed for the bed, reaching for the buttons of his shirt as he walked. His eyes expressed his approval with the billowy ivory confection Merry had donned while she'd waited for him. "God, you're beautiful."

Two years of familiarity had not dimmed the pleasure Merry found in his sincerely uttered compliments. Grant still had the ability to make her feel like the most desirable woman in the world—even when she suspected that she was beginning to resemble a lace-covered blimp. She smiled lovingly as he swiftly stripped off the rest of his clothes before joining her on the bed. Familiarity had not made his firm, tanned body any less beautiful to her, either.

"Did you fix Melinda's tape player?" she asked as he slipped beneath the sheets, already reaching for her.

"Mmm," he murmured affirmatively, snuggling his face into her hair. "Amazing what new batteries can do for rock and roll."

Her hands gliding down his sleek bare back, Merry tried to concentrate on the conversation. "It . . . it took you all this time to change batteries?"

"Uh-uh. She couldn't figure out the answer to an algebra problem."

"You made her work it out herself, I trust."

"Of course," he replied with mild indignation, his lips moving toward the deep scooped neckline of her nightgown. "I just helped a little."

"Sure you did," Merry murmured skeptically, knowing that both the twins had Grant wrapped firmly around their little fingers. And he loved every minute of it.

Grant enfolded her with both arms and hugged her tightly, his heart overflowing with love and contentment. What had he done, he wondered as their baby lazily kicked him in the stomach, to deserve such happiness? Barely holding back the unexpected rush of emotion, he managed to smile and speak teasingly to Merry's rounded belly. "Go back to sleep, kid," he said rather hoarsely. "Your mom and I would like a little privacy now."

"I love you, Grant." Merry's voice quavered as if she'd sensed his sudden vulnerability and had been greatly touched by it.

"I love you." He kissed her deeply, his fingers going to the fastening of her gown.

"It's going to be hectic for the next couple of weeks," she warned him in a husky whisper. "Matt will be staying here for three days before and two days after the wedding. Marsha and Tim will be gone for two weeks on their honeymoon, so you and I will both be extra busy with work. And Chip's graduating in two weeks and you promised to take him camping the weekend after his graduation. The twins have finals coming up—Lord, I can't believe they'll be entering the eleventh grade in the fall! And mmph!"

"Merry," Grant said patiently, his hand firmly over her mouth, "I know what's scheduled for the next few weeks. Why do you feel it necessary to discuss it at this particular moment?"

Smiling ruefully, she pushed his hand away. "I guess I'm still surprised that you willingly took all this on," she admitted. "No regrets, Grant?"

"No regrets, Merry." He kissed her, sliding her nightgown away from her creamy shoulders. "Not one. I love you so much. And I've never been happier in my life. Why should I have any regrets?"

"You're right." Merry smiled, then gasped as she arched into the mouth that had closed over the tip of her breast. "You're a very lucky man, Grant Bryant."

His tongue flicked lightly over the hardening rose tip. "Yes, Merry Bryant, I am."

And he allowed no more talk—and no more interruptions until morning.

This month's irresistible novels from

THE LADY IN THE MIRROR by Judith Arnold

Bachelor Arms

Ex-cop Clint McCreary had come to L.A. from New York for just one reason: to find his runaway teenage sister. Not to have his heart held hostage by Jessie Gale, a lovely luscious blonde who managed a shelter for runaways…

LOOK INTO MY EYES by Glenda Sanders

Secret Fantasies

After the death of her fiancé, Holly Bennett thinks her dreams are shattered, but then she meets mysterious Craig Ford. They share an overwhelming attraction, only Craig can't promise Holly anything, because he has no memories of his previous life. Will his past put an end to their future?

THE LAWMAN by Vicki Lewis Thompson

Urban Cowboys

From the moment sexy Leigh Singleton met cynical cop Joe Gilardini, she knew he was the man for her. His son, Kyle, was an added bonus. But could she help Joe come to terms with his troubled past? And could she convince him she wasn't the criminal he was seeking?

CAUSE FOR CELEBRATION by Gina Wilkins

Overwhelmed by work, Merry James was in no mood for a party. But since theme parties were her livelihood, she was determined to look on the bright side. After the appearance of sexy Grant Bryant, the man she assumed was her temporary secretary, things were certainly looking up. Was a steamy office romance on the cards?

Spoil yourself next month
with these four novels from

TIMELESS LOVE by Judith Arnold

Bachelor Arms

Why did Hope Henley flee in terror from Apartment 1-G—
straight into the path of Morgan Delacourt's car? Surviving that
experience was one thing...accepting Morgan's generous offer
of convalescence at his home was quite another. Suddenly, Hope
found herself believing in all sorts of crazy notions...like
destined, timeless love with sexy Morgan...

CHARLIE ALL NIGHT by Jennifer Crusie

Dumped by her boyfriend and dropped from prime time, radio
producer Allie McGuffey had nowhere to go but up. So she
planned to make temporary DJ Charlie Tenniel a household
name. But that was the last thing on Charlie's mind. He shunned
fame. He just wanted to relax, play good records and make love
to Allie—despite her objections!

PRIVATE PASSIONS by JoAnn Ross

Secret Fantasies

By day, Desiree Dupree is an investigative reporter. But at night,
she pens sexy, intimate love stories. Lately, mysterious Roman
Falconer has been playing a starring role in her fantasies—*and*
she's investigating him. Something scary is going on in New
Orleans and Roman's novels seem to contain the answers...

A BURNING TOUCH by Patricia Ryan

The nights in Mansfield are hot—an arsonist is terrorizing the
town. But that's nothing compared to the heat Detective Jamie
Keegan experiences after one look into the lovely eyes of India
Cook. She's offered her services as a psychic to the police
department, but cynical Jamie doesn't believe a word. What can
she do to convince him of her special talents?

One to Another

A year's supply of Mills & Boon® novels— absolutely FREE!

Would you like to win a year's supply of heartwarming and passionate romances? Well, you can and they're FREE! Simply complete the missing word competition below and send it to us by 28th February 1997. The first 5 correct entries picked after the closing date will win a year's supply of Mills & Boon romance novels (six books every month—worth over £150). What could be easier?

PAPER	B A C K	WARDS
ARM		MAN
PAIN		ON
SHOE		TOP
FIRE		MAT
WAIST		HANGER
BED		BOX
BACK		AGE
RAIN		FALL
CHOPPING		ROOM

Please turn over for details of how to enter ☞

How to enter...

There are ten missing words in our grid overleaf.
Each of the missing words must connect up with the
words on either side to make a new word—e.g.
PAPER-BACK-WARDS. As you find each one, write it in
the space provided, we've done the first one for you!

When you have found all the words, don't forget to fill in
your name and address in the space provided below and
pop this page into an envelope (you don't even need a
stamp) and post it today. Hurry—competition ends
28th February 1997.

**Mills & Boon® One to Another
FREEPOST
Croydon
Surrey
CR9 3WZ**